I0578523

Demon Curse

MARIE FLYNN

Small Fish
publishing

Small Fish Publishing
USA

This is a work of fiction. Names, characters, places, and incidents either are the products of the author's imagination or are used fictitiously. Any resemblance to actual persons, living or dead, businesses, companies, events, or locales is entirely coincidental.

Copyright © 2023, 2021 Marie Flynn

All rights reserved. This book or parts thereof may not be reproduced in any form, stored in any retrieval system, or transmitted in any form by any means—electronic, mechanical, photocopy, recording, or otherwise.
First edition
Cover design by Stephanie Flynn
ISBN ebook: 9781952372278
ISBN paperback: 9781952372308
ISBN hardcover: 9781952372315
ISBN large print paperback: 9781952372797

Also By Marie Flynn

Demon Cat Chronicles series
Demon Curse
Twice Cursed

If you like steamy romance mixed in with your paranormal tales, check out Marie Flynn's other name, Stephanie Flynn!

Prologue

Identified

Andras

I FINALLY HAD AN answer to give the king, which meant my months toiling at the surface among the humans was paying off. During this precarious time, the king would be pleased, so I eagerly popped through a portal down to Hell City, an underground metropolis far too subterranean for human detection. The place was named long before I was born, but my suggestions for a less primitive name were brushed aside as 'too intellectually superior and unnecessarily pompous.' I shrugged it off.

A sense of relief always washed over me when I passed through. Humans didn't react well to those different from themselves. They couldn't even play nice with variances in skin tone and hair texture. Imagine how they'd react to us. Before it was pitchforks and disjointed fear stories, but the damage they could do was limited. Now I supposed they'd use weaponized drones and a military with an arsenal that made the rest of the world nervous. It made us nervous, honestly.

But down here, the demons born without the ability to glamour themselves into a humanoid appearance could live in peace. Demons with the ability to glamour, like me, were assigned work at the surface, but since glamouring required considerable energy, most demons, myself included, released our glamours around each other and in private. So I did, changing from a passable human to my natural size. Ducking through doorways was annoying sometimes, especially since the king was exceptionally short—by human standards.

The stone hallway was dank and dark with burning torches lighting the eerie path, part of the required effect. Since humans never came down here, I thought it was unnecessarily pompous, but hey, I didn't get to make the decisions around here.

I bent down and knocked on Corson's office door, officially titled The King of Hell. 'The' was an important distinction, in case a future apprentice king were to be chosen, the original king needed the distinction. And despite the title, it was an elected position. To have a chance at the crown, the best demon had to hone his skills in combat against the Great Enemy and prove him or herself in strategy. Mastery of both swords and pyromancy were needed. Being a skilled shot with firearms was useful, especially when framing humans for a hit on the surface.

But with the current affairs topside, no one else wanted to be king. Not even me, and I was currently his number one.

"Enter," the gruff reply penetrated the thick ancient door.

I ducked through the door. Corson and I had been playmates at school, and with our friendly relationship intact hundreds of years later, the king dropped his glamour, shrinking him from a still-short five-and-a-quarter feet tall down to his natural four-and-a-pinch feet tall. Add a bright red corkscrew tail swishing behind him, and a pair of curled horns on his head no bigger than a goat's, intimidating he was not. But the power in that small package commanded respect.

The King of Hell returned to his work at his desk, hopping up onto the chair, and sliding reading glasses onto the narrow bridge of his nose.

We demons had plenty of entertainment, but we had to keep close tabs on the humans, so we tracked their news diligently. Human taste rubbed off on some of us. The king's office was typical of any corporate headquarters above ground, except the plate glass window overlooked a city shrouded in permanent night, and only the lights of the buildings cast a glow. The closest human equivalent would be a polar night in Norway, and Hell was just about as cold, or so the humans had complained. The temperature was a common misconception, but the cold didn't bother us any.

I approached the glossy wood desk, dwarfing my boss and friend. "I've come with good news."

The king craned his neck up to meet my eye. "Have you confirmed the correct human?"

My natural demon shape stood over seven feet tall with iridescent purple scales, very much like a flightless dragon. I'd inherited that sweet gene from my mother. Damn her soul. My tail, however, was long and sometimes it went where I didn't want it. With a thump of Corson's desk and a rattle of his lamp chain, I apologized to my friend.

Corson frowned. "We can't all have long, luxurious tails, now, can we? Don't worry about it. Now, what did you find out?"

I clicked on the television mounted to the ceiling in the corner and caught the end of the morning program. When the familiar face appeared, I nodded. "This is him."

The screen split between the Channel 9 news anchor at the station and the interviewee in his plush office. Nick Barnes wore a healthy grin, and he oozed charisma while he stroked his jaw. He wore a tailored suit with a nice tie. His hair reached chin length and was styled with more care than most human males bothered with. The man lived on the twentieth floor of his own skyscraper.

At a glance, he'd make a great demon.

I'd spend months with the man personally, who I first thought was just rich, handsome, and arrogant, which were the qualities that drew me to him. Eventually, I discovered what lay beneath the facade, a broken man who survived a nightmare childhood. He had more issues than National Geographic, and just as much carnage and beauty.

The King of Hell removed his reading glasses and squinted at the screen.

The woman news anchor said, "Internal medicine experts are calling Anycillin a miracle drug. Do you have a comment for us?"

The man of the hour beamed and flicked his nicely styled hair. If I could grow some, I'd want Nick's wavy layers. Enough women swooned over him for it. Or maybe it was the multi-million-dollar company and the penthouse condo.

Nah, definitely the hair.

Unfortunately for them, Nick was taken.

Nick said with heartfelt sympathy, "Busy families can't afford to have Mom or Dad sick for weeks, losing work. Our elderly citizens don't have weeks of their lives left to waste in a hospital bed. I dedicated my life to helping these people, all people, you included." The news anchor grinned. "One dose of one simple pill can eradicate most known bacterial infections, or at least, that's how my scientist explains it to me." Nick Barnes chuckled, the charismatic bastard. I wasn't jealous at all. Nope.

The news anchor blushed and tossed her stiff hair. "It sure sounds like a miracle. Thank you, Mr. Barnes. Coming up next, Ted Bastion and Novalite Pharmaceuticals have a new antibiotic that's going to change the future of medical care. Back to you, Stu."

"He's an arrogant ass, isn't he?" the king asked.

"Yes, he is." I clicked off the television. "But that's his son, sir. I'm sure of it."

"The ones with big heads are always the worst to tame." The king scratched the wisps on his scalp. "When you feel he's ready, introduce him to our world, but you must be certain of his cooperation. I cannot stress that enough."

"Understood, sir. It's an honor to fight for Hell at this pivotal moment—history in the making."

The king tilted his face up and frowned. "It's always an honor to fight for Hell. Don't tell me you've considered switching sides." He raised his brows in challenge, but it was a rhetorical statement. The Great Enemy would kill me on sight if they could without instigating another war.

Just to be safe, I reassured him, anyway. "Never, sir. I meant riveting things are coming to pass."

"Indeed. Suit up." The king sighed. "I'm being summoned by Ted Bastion. You know where to find me."

The king activated his glamour, shifting into a Caucasian human who was shorter than the average man, but he didn't need height to command more respect from humans. And I initiated my own glamour with a strain on my skin, shrinking my size to a passable human. I teleported to a nearby Hell portal, but before crossing the threshold, I checked my watch.

Ah, hell. I was late to update my cohort on the new developments.

I

One Question

Nick

IN ANY MOMENT IN my life, I never would've said everything was perfect, but somehow, through perseverance, luck, or insurmountable debt, it happened. Tonight, the final piece was fitting into position, revealing the beautiful image I'd been fighting uphill my whole life to see—a fiancée.

Lauren Hamil and I had been dating for longer than was customary before becoming engaged, and our ages—early thirties for her and hitting forty in a few coughs for me—reflected I was a little late. But I had excuses.

Well, one big one.

NBB Pharmaceuticals was my baby. I'd bought it out with other people's money, and I'd nurtured it, watered it, filled it with hopes and dreams. In a few days, I had a meeting for a life-changing contract, and I would do anything to make it happen. I'd gone too far. I'd sacrificed too much.

I couldn't fail.

Dad's words from my childhood echoed in my head, but I brushed them away. No, Dad, very soon you were going to eat your words. My presentation was ready. My spreadsheets were in a line, and my charts were pretty. I was all set. All I needed was the support of the woman who'd been at my beck and call for three years.

We hadn't moved in together yet, but that was the logical next step after tonight. Lauren probably would've preferred a more public venue for this, but funds were limited. I had to give everything I had to NBB, so even though I looked the part, and I lived in a penthouse—it was above my own company, so really a cost-saving measure—I didn't have what I appeared to have.

Sometimes appearances were all that was needed.

I set up a small round table in my living room—complete with a white tablecloth, shiny white plates, cloth napkins, and sparkling silverware. I added a vase I'd nabbed from my mom's vast collection and tossed in a grocery store bouquet of white flowers. Candles were lit, food was in the warmer, and then I waited.

For her.

And then I got bored. I went over to my aquarium, an impressive two-thousand-gallon saltwater reef, filled with fish and both small and large polyp corals, and of course, some softies. If I'd had the extra cash at the time, I would've gone with acrylic, just for the record. Tuna blue light shimmied over the fingers of coral, and soft tentacles danced in the flow. Even the tang police would've patted me on the back for proper stocking. After years of searching, I'd collected the elusive gem tang, the emperor angelfish, and I even knew a guy who knew a guy who got me a golden basslet.

To me, this display was perfect, a seamless blend of elegance and the raw power of nature, easy to please and uncomplicated, sort of. The fish cavorted across the front of the glass, wove through the arches in the rockwork, and congregated near me. I wanted to think they greeted me as a friend, but they were only expecting food, and as long as I provided them with a comfortable home and plenty of sustenance, they never asked for anything more.

I couldn't understand why Lauren had no interest. But she had interests I didn't like either. And that was okay. We had mutual respect, our own interests, and a few shared ones, too. It was a healthy relationship. One I wanted to last forever.

The door buzzed with a visitor, and my heart leaped into my throat in anticipation. I straightened my tie, smoothed my styled locks—just in case—and checked my breath. I'd tasted the food while cooking it, but I didn't smell wretched or anything.

I smiled in preparation and opened the door. Lauren stood in the doorway, smoldering gaze on her painted features, brunette hair cascading over her narrow shoulders, and the well-lifted rack front and center of a tight-fitting black dress. I loved her boobs. They were the definition of divine, if I were a believer in that sort of thing.

"You called?" Lauren asked with a steamy husk in her voice.

I planned on making use of that voice later. But first, the main event. "I have a special dinner planned." I swung my arm toward the impressive display for an intimate evening.

Lauren sashayed past me, and her heels clattered against my hardwood floors. I couldn't wait to have those heels over my shoulder. She rested her hands on the backrest of a chair. "What's all this?"

She was impressed, thankfully. "You'll see. Have a seat." I assisted her into a seated position, like gentlemen in the movies did, and I headed into the kitchen. Donning oven mitts, I lifted the casserole out of the oven and set it on the burners. I uncovered the ham and Swiss dish and inhaled a satisfied whiff.

It was perfect. Smiling to myself, I collected the salad from the fridge and carried both out to the living room, catching a glance at my fish, and I settled them on the edge of the table. I didn't need the candles to get knocked over and burn the place down. I wouldn't be able to rescue my fish from such a blaze.

Lauren set her phone aside and leaned toward the dish. "What's that?"

"Ham and Swiss."

"Like the country?" Lauren wasn't much for cooking, but she did travel a lot. Her family had money, and Lauren knew nothing else. Our backgrounds couldn't have been more different, but sometimes opposites attracted.

I caught another glance at her ample chest. "The cheese."

"It looks weird, but I'll try it."

She served herself salad first and a dollop of the casserole. I made myself a generous helping of the first, and a filling serving of the second. I sat down to eat with her, both of us unfolding the napkins for our laps and choosing the right forks for the entrée. Besides the hum of my wave makers, the penthouse was quiet.

"What's the special occasion?" Lauren cleaned a bite off her fork and chewed, focusing on my culinary skills. They weren't much, nothing like my mother's, but I needed to do this for her.

"We can get to that in a minute. How was your day?"

"Fine. You're being weird."

I thought I hid my nerves well, but it didn't matter. I loved this woman. "Tomorrow night is my family's annual Thanksgiving birthday dinner, and I'm looking forward to it this year."

"Why?" Lauren took another bite. Seemed my dish was palatable. Other than the calorie count, it wasn't half-bad. "Your family is always mean to you. I don't know why you go."

I couldn't wipe the smile off my face. "I have a reason to this year."

"What's that?"

She was practically begging me to do it. In the middle of my meal, I couldn't wait any longer. I folded up my napkin and set it aside. Climbing to my feet, I pulled the box out of my pocket and kneeled. I opened it before she could say a word. "Lauren—"

Her hand went to her chest. The other dropped her fork. It hit the edge of her plate and tumbled to the hardwood, Swiss cheese and all. Lauren just stared.

"We've been through everything together—ski trips to the Alps, dinner parties with members of Congress, and even golfing in the Caribbean. Through it all, you've been by my side and supported me as much as I eagerly support you. There is no other woman on this earth for me. You're it. You're my everything. Will you marry me?"

Lauren didn't look at me. She stared at the ring, though. That had to be a good sign. "Nick, I don't know what to say."

"The customary answer is 'yes', but I'll take an 'okay' or 'of course' or even 'duh, idiot.'" I gave her a lopsided grin while I freed the ring from the box and reached for her left hand.

Lauren pulled away, and my heart leaped into my throat like a punching bag hit by a heavyweight.

"I don't think you have the right idea here." She curled that hand up against the other like some sort of shield.

"I know exactly what I'm doing. I want to marry you. Since the moment I laid eyes on you, I knew you were the one. We just had to get here first, and now I'm ready. If you're not, I can wait." My chest squeezed. "I can wait," I said slowly, hedging against what I feared most.

"I don't think that's a good idea."

I exhaled and rose. "What do you mean? Talk to me, Lauren. What's the holdup? I love you."

Lauren balled up her napkin and tossed it onto the table, carelessly landing on the candle flame. I peeled it free and gave her my full attention again. "It's too small."

I coughed. "What?"

"I can't be seen by my friends wearing that. It's too small."

The ring. That was somewhat of a relief. "Then we can get you a bigger one, eventually."

"That's the problem, Nick. It's always 'eventually.' Face it, you're broke, and that doesn't work for me."

I frowned. "I've always been broke. Why was it okay before?"

She touched my lapel. "I thought you were going to be someone, but I can't wait anymore. Sorry." Lauren headed for the door but paused with her hand on the knob. She called over her shoulder, "The cheese was good."

And then she was gone.

The weight of the world crushed me from all directions. I couldn't breathe; I couldn't move. I didn't think I could stay standing much longer. All I could do was throw the ring away, and I tossed it carelessly, just how Lauren tossed our love away. It landed in the saltwater tank with a soft plop and shimmied to the aragonite sand bed.

My fish would appreciate it more, anyway. The only sound was the hum of my wave makers, trying to lull me into a gentle embrace, but the allure of my fish didn't help this time. My knees gave out, and I hit the floor with a crack. I would feel that...eventually. Right now, I was numb.

I was everything Lauren said.

Everything my father said.

A failure.

2

Thanksgiving Birthday

TEXTS HAD GONE UNANSWERED, so I attempted to sleep on it, but I didn't catch more than a wink. All night I held out hope Lauren would show up today, having taken the time to think about it, too. As I lowered myself onto a seat, I'd received the dreaded text. '*We're over, Nick.*'

Sitting at my parents' dining room table, I used every ounce of my strength to ignore that message and hold myself together. Lauren hadn't arrived to help me save face, and cows with dead beady eyes stared from towels, framed prints, refrigerator magnets, and even the salt and pepper shakers. But the cows with swinging tails marking the seconds bothered me the most. Yes, plural. There was no comforting hum of wave makers here. Stella Barnes, my mother, owned five cow clocks, three of which hung in the kitchen, and none of them were perfectly in unison.

The off-rhythm ticking was driving me mad, and that was before considering the present company.

Flatware clattered against an eclectic mix of plastic and porcelain bowls, containing a hearty selection of the finest American food: juicy steak, mashed potatoes and gravy, peas, salad, biscuits, sugar cookies, and wine. No one could pry the butter from my mom's hands. I tried to reason with her once, concerned over her heart, but that was the last time. Only two things insulted Stella Barnes: not showing up for dinner or not eating enough. Exact quantities were unknown and appeared to vary on the occasion. Mashed potatoes passed in a circle around the table, and I scooped myself a small serving to appease her.

I'd rather run before the questions began.

My older brother, Chris Barnes, darted his eyes between me, Mom, and our father, Dennis, as if waiting for the obvious elephant in the room to stand up and flip the table for fun. If I had a mighty trunk of my own, I'd do it myself just to drown out the chorus of ticking and save Dennis the effort.

Every year, Mom insisted on a family dinner to celebrate two of their birthdays—hers and Chris's, which were near Thanksgiving. And every year, the favorite son brought his wife while I attempted to bring a date. Mom's disappointment in Lauren skipping this year showed with each smack of her spoon, clank of flatware against her plate, and thump of her glass. I wasn't taking the blame for this year's impending fight, so I ate peacefully, ignoring that fat elephant in the corner, smirking at me in anticipation.

I was lucid enough to understand the elephant wasn't real. When I was a child, I'd named the elephant Odie, short for Odysseus, but Mom always thought my cute imaginary friend was named after the cartoon dog. I'd never bothered to correct her. Unlike me, the elephant never aged, never left, and always lurked in the corner, unhelpfully staring.

Mom cleared her throat. *Here we go.* "Is Lauren sick today?" Her sweet tone and gentle smile, wrinkling the corners of her eyes, didn't fool me. Complementing the mop of unruly gray hair on her head, a well-worn cow-printed apron hugged her curves. She hadn't bothered to take it off before sitting. Stella Barnes was the epitome of grandma, less the grandkids. That was Chris's job.

"I don't think so," I said, swallowing a bite of fluffy potatoes as a delay tactic. All I wanted was a meal in peace and to get out the door with nothing broken. At least the potatoes were great. Too bad the company couldn't be.

"Is she working?" Mom pressed.

I lifted my glass of water and sipped. After this, I might have to indulge in a rum and Coke night, which totally threw off my gym routine.

"You're stalling." Dennis sawed at his steak like it was still alive. The old man—I never thought of my father as Father—was a low-risk low-reward stubborn man, retired from a proud plumbing career, whose abdominal projection increased each year proportionately with the increase in beer consumption. He'd earned the family a survivable wage and always held hard labor to the highest esteem. Anything else wasn't *work*, like my history of less-than-stellar start-ups. Those were just the irresponsible gambles of an immature boy. I had given up mending our rocky relationship long ago. All I hoped for was a mutual truce, but now Odie the elephant replaced the usual smirk for a grin of anticipation.

Ignoring Dennis's provocation, I answered her point-blank to tear off the bandage. "We broke up."

Mom's smile never faltered, as if she, too, didn't accept those words. They hadn't sunk in for me, either. Mom blinked. "What do you mean?"

Digging deeper into my—I glanced at Dennis—*failed* love life was only going to lead to me embarrassing myself. I changed the subject to keep the anguish tucked away beneath my suit and tie. "I have some exciting news about work."

"Now you're deflecting," Dennis said and stuffed a dripping bite into his mouth.

"Does this news affect Chris's position?" Mom asked, meeting the golden child's eye with a blank smile.

"Not exactly, no."

My pudgy older brother managed NBB's marketing department, and as of now, his job wouldn't change, but my meeting was tomorrow for a contract that would change my life forever. And the world. But it wasn't a sure thing, and I didn't want to get anyone's hopes up, but I needed to show them they had something to be proud of. "But it will be great for—"

"It doesn't matter then," Mom said sharply, interrupting me.

I clenched my teeth. Her narrow focus made no sense. "Why do you only care about who's sharing my bed? Why do you insist I have someone to sleep with? Are you worried I'm too old for kids? Newsflash, kids are not in my future. Or are you worried I might be a closeted gay man? Is my sex life that important to you? Would you like a Venn diagram?" I could make the circles all pretty.

Mom gasped.

Chris's eyebrows lifted while he stared at his plate and shuffled peas around. He only remained silent when he wasn't in the line of fire. When we were children, Chris had plenty to say, and Dennis always used the old axiom 'boys will be boys', dismissing my complaints. As an adult, I had no qualms about ignoring my brother's comments, until I had been guilted into giving him a job.

With calloused hands, Dennis gripped the edge of the table and leaned forward. "Don't you speak to your mother like that."

"She asked." I sipped from my glass of water, feeling a bit smug.

"I did no such thing," Mom countered with a hand over her heart, mouth still hanging open.

This was going nowhere good, so I shifted the attention to my brother. "What about you, Chris? Where's Cyndi?"

My older brother shook extra pepper into his peas. "One of her coworkers called in sick, so she's covering."

"Now that's just sweet of her," Mom cooed. "Tell Cyndi we missed her very much. Make sure you take leftovers home for her."

"I will. Thanks, Mom."

Mom's love for my sister-in-law's career never made sense. She fawned over Cyndi's work as if she were a doctor traveling to countries in conflict zones and treating endemic diseases. No, Cyndi Barnes worked retail, risking her sleep for people's shopping discounts or need for last-minute fuzzy sweaters. Neither Dennis nor Mom approved of my career path, which frankly baffled me. My work delivered medicine to the sick, so, arguably, I was closer to the battlefront than Cyndi ever would be.

The lazy family cat rubbed up against my pant leg under the table. I shivered. Cats were not my thing—leaving fur everywhere, vomiting on places, smearing feces on the floor. And their sharp eyes always held more intelligence than they deserved, as if some higher being was in there, mocking me. Just no. I shifted my leg and tried to shoo it away. As a fish guy, I grimaced at the orange fur on my leg and the static cling. Just great. Hopefully, my fur brush was still in the car. I swatted at the patch of fur, and a torrent of orange kicked up and floated.

"Nicky!" Mom scolded.

I picked every last piece of fur off my pants manually and searched for a safe place to rest my legs out of reach of the cat, but no such luck. This meal couldn't get any worse.

Dennis stood and headed to the kitchen. A moment later, he returned with another bottle of beer. I wagered today's gathering would be a six-beer night.

"Cyndi is an amazing girl, Chris." Mom smiled with a sparkle in her eye. That look meant the words were sincere, but that look was never directed my way. As I thought about it, Mom met my eye, and the smile slid away. "Nicky, I only want to see you settled and happy. Why did you dump this one? Lauren seemed like a nice girl."

Chris's brows rose once again. Lauren might've rejected my proposal, but I wanted to defend her against whatever was running through his idiot head. Regardless, I was tired of this stupid reputation they bestowed upon me. If I tell them the truth, perhaps, just perhaps, they'd lay off my love life for good. "I didn't dump her."

Chris looked me in the eye. "Then what did you do?"

"I didn't do anything." I pointedly glared at each shocked face at the table, and Dennis tilted his head as if he didn't hear right.

Mom's fork froze in the air. "Are you saying *she* dumped *you*? I bet it's because you're never around for her. It's because you're never around, isn't it, Nicky? I always said—"

"It happened, and it's over," I cut off her insulting psychoanalysis and piled on the sarcasm. "I admit it. I'm not perfect."

My sarcasm was lost on Dennis. Always was. "Pride and greed are clogging up the plumbing in your brain. You lust after things you don't deserve, and that NBB building is just a giant symbol for the gluttony you live for. You're *not* perfect, and you should be worried about your downward spiral."

Dennis was the last man someone would expect to read the Bible, and even if he had—I'm not convinced—he'd never attended church services, as far as I was aware, so this was a bit out there even for him. I was purely a non-believer, because if a benevolent god existed, I wouldn't be in business.

I barked out a dark laugh at the ridiculousness. "I'm perfectly content with my life and all its numerous sins, Dad. Thanks for the judgment."

If only Odie would lift his lazy bulk from the corner, waddle over, and free me from all this. He looked as if he were fighting back laughter. Happy to entertain, as always.

Chris lifted a wedge of biscuit to make his point. "Dad's right. You're a priest's wet dream."

Mom gasped.

"I'm not in their target age group." I bit back a chuckle.

"Nicky!" Mom shouted.

Dad railed into me with another set of insults and reminded me to respect my mother, et cetera, and so on. Not one word flew at Chris for insulting me first.

When everyone calmed down, my brother continued, "I meant if you would've done whatever Lauren asked, and I'm going to go out on a limb here, but by being available"—Mom nodded—"and having normal work hours, she just might've been here tonight. I have a normal job and a loving wife. One of those things allows me to have the other."

"Correlation does not mean causation." Blank stares. It wasn't fun if they didn't understand. "You're a hypocrite, Chris. Remember who signs your checks the next time you insist on taking a jab at my lifestyle." I dipped my biscuit into my gravy pool, but my appetite quickly waned.

Chris's face flushed red. "I like my job, okay? I'm only trying to help. Do you feel better now?"

There was nothing as satisfying as watching your brother struggle to eat humble pie.

"You don't need to apologize, honey," Mom said, selecting a cookie off the serving plate.

I wanted this conversation to end, but I didn't want to roll over and take it like the twelve-year-old me used to. "I don't complain about my life, so I'd appreciate if everyone laid off my back about it. And I don't need pity. Lauren wasn't that special." A spear to the gut told me that was a lie, but Lauren didn't want to discuss it, and I couldn't think about it right now.

"Pity?" Dennis repeated, cracking the lid off his fourth beer. Not enough for inebriation, but enough for belligerent. *Here we go again.* "We raised you to be a better man. We worked hard to show you what being a good man meant. But all you've ever done was run your mouth, sneak off behind our backs, and throw away every piece of advice we ever gave you. We wanted you to find a woman who could guide you in ways we couldn't. Pity isn't the word I'd use. You're going to hell, and there's nothing we can do about it any longer."

My blood boiled, and the urge to defend myself trumped keeping the peace. "You're right. Instead of being your perfect son, following in daddy's footsteps, I decided to use my head rather than my hands for a living. What did it get me? I own a pharmaceutical company that saves lives. I employ hundreds of workers in the city. I fly internationally to shake hands with politicians, and I have best friends in lobbying. No matter how successful I am, it's never enough because I don't have a woman on my arm while I do it. Tell me, *Dad*, what is enough for you?"

Dennis's face scrunched with contained fury. "You failed before, and you'll fail again."

I leaned forward. "I'm tenacious, and I'm not a quitter."

Odie's shoulders shook with silent chuckles. Jackass.

Dennis's fury darkened his whole head. He matched Mom's wine now. "It means you're a failure, you ungrateful, stubborn bastard. And it's only a matter of time before history repeats itself. Don't you ever learn?"

Forks clattered, and Mom gasped. "Language, honey. Watch your language!"

Dennis ignored her pointless plea, not for the first time, and I said, "I'm curious where this perception of being an ungrateful bastard comes from."

"You came into our home tonight—" Dennis started.

"Invited," I corrected. "I was explicitly invited, and I didn't want to come, but I thought Lauren would join me. Because she didn't, now I've been subjected to my entire life being dissected and thrown in my face."

"Then you shouldn't have come."

"If I didn't, you'd be hunting me down and cursing me to your god." I tossed my napkin on the table. "Remember last year? I still have those voicemails." It was a string of insults and guilt, because I didn't accept the invite, then I was late, then I didn't show. I never would've come today if I knew Lauren wouldn't have shown.

Mom gasped again. One more shocking outburst and she'd faint.

Dennis bristled, arms and fists clenching for a fight. "Don't you dare interrupt me, boy. We raised you here in this house, but we get nothing but disrespect. The oxygen must be so thin in that ivory tower of yours, it's affecting your ability to be human."

The cat made another pass at my leg. I hid a cringe and said, "Concrete and steel."

"Excuse me?" Dennis's fists were balls of iron, ready to swing drunkenly.

Nothing good would come from staying. I rose and tucked in my chair. "Thank you for the meal, Mom."

"What? No! Where are you...?" Mom whined while I brought my plate to the sink.

Dennis met me at the doorway, hands braced against the frame for support. "Get out of my house, you bastard! You're no longer welcome here, and I never want to hear from you again." He called over his shoulder, "Hear that, honey? Nick is not welcome here ever again."

I shook my head and smiled. Perhaps coming today wasn't a mistake after all. "Thank you."

Dennis frowned, not understanding.

I added, "Thank you for making this easy. I'm happy to leave and never come back."

"But, but Dennis! Nicky, you can't. What about...?" Mom's frantic babbling was only about one thing, and she looked at him with true worry.

So I finished for her. "Don't worry yourself, Mom. Chris still has a job." Because Chris's well-being was all they'd ever cared about. I brushed past Dennis and through the dining room.

"Now, hold on. Nicky, we all let tempers get out of hand. Let's sit down and finish the meal like civilized people," Mom pleaded. "I haven't served the cake yet. We still have to sing. I love the singing."

"I guess I checked my civility at the door." I glared at Dennis, but the man only swigged from his beer. "I'll see myself out and grab my civility on the way. The meal was good, Mom. Chris, say 'hi' to Cyndi for me."

Before any more protesting, I closed the front door on my way out. Disowned by my family at thirty-nine years old. Stupid, useless elephant. Always ruining the party.

Not only did they take credit for me getting to leave them behind, but now I had a clear head. I wasn't crushed, destroyed, embarrassed by Lauren rejecting me. I never should've lost my focus in the first place. My parents were always wrong about everything. I was going to save the world eventually.

To do that, I was going to secure this contract, and now I had the confidence and focus to do it.

Spite was a hell of a motivator.

3

The Future

Fiber optic speeds made video capabilities more than sufficient for online meetings these days, but this was top secret—officially, unofficially?—I didn't know, but the non-disclosure agreement I'd signed to simply discuss this deal was ironclad. Prepared and ready, I nervously flew down to Atlanta for the biggest business deal of my life.

Good thing Dennis's misplaced insults and Mom's deflections interrupted my spilling the beans on this. I wasn't going to give them enough details to risk the contract regardless, but a few nibbles to elevate their opinions would've been satisfying.

As my marketing manager, Chris was better at the graphs than I was, but he didn't belong here. These were scientists who needed to believe in *me*, and Chris's doubting commentary wasn't welcome. Besides, this wasn't his wheelhouse. I didn't need consumers to be tricked into choosing our product over the next guy's. As if I needed another excuse, the success here today had to be mine and only mine. I left my brother in the dark on this entirely, and it wasn't just spite.

I clicked to reveal the next slide of my presentation while high-ranking people watched curiously from their seats around the long wood table. Several were members of the medical board here at the Centers for Disease Control and Prevention, and one was a director from the Department of Defense. Their job was to verify if my plan was viable. Since I wasn't a scientist, I'd employed the skills of my actual scientist, Dr. Tyler Gibson. The man was a microbiologist and a certifiable genius. No, I didn't make that up. We'd crafted the medical portion of the presentation together, and I'd memorized the speech and answers to common questions. Dr. Gibson assured me my answers made sense, but I thought it was gibberish. I didn't get where I was by facts alone.

The next image appeared on the screen, and brilliant minds around the table turned silent. Some of them gasped softly, and I took that as a good sign.

"They're green," a man in his sixties said, astonished. Other than his curled gray mustache, he and his other white-lab-coated brethren were nearly indistinguishable.

I relished their amazement. I fed off it. "Using the standardized Gram stain test, bacteria can only appear purple or pink," I explained, as if they didn't believe the images. "These photos have not been altered in any way. What you're seeing makes no sense, isn't possible...until now. At NBB, our research team was able to create a new strain altogether—one that breaks the walls of impossibility and opens doors to new opportunity."

"But how?" another man asked. Still in a white lab coat. They all just looked the same.

I brushed the hair back away from my face and gave them a charming smile. "For that, you'd have to ask my doctor. I'm just the money guy."

A few chuckles eased my nerves, and I changed the slide. "As you can see here, this is the new, atypical bacterium, resistant to all known antibiotics, including macrolides. Just like you wanted."

Another indistinguishable old man in a white lab coat asked, "Who is your lead scientist?"

I was proud to show off my man. "Dr. Tyler Gibson."

Brows rose around the table. That same man said, "We offered him a position here at the CDC, but he turned it down."

Dr. Gibson had told me he wanted more money, which I didn't fault him for. A man's gotta eat. "Then you know exactly the genius we're working with."

"He is as brilliant as you say, but how is this creation of yours resistant to antibiotics?" the curled mustache man said.

"I'm the man behind Anycillin. It's been tested against our most universal antibiotic and everything currently on the market. It survives like a cockroach after an apocalypse."

"Are you a religious man, Mr. Barnes?" Curled Mustache asked.

Well, that was a trick question. Would a 'no' lose their respect or gain it? Would a 'yes' result in the opposite reaction? From my parents' terror at my unending blasphemy, I erred on the side that followed my principles. "I believe in telling the truth, and that truth is I believe in science, just like you fine people. My example was merely that, a graphic image to reinforce just how invincible this bacterium is." I pointed over my shoulder at the green-stained wiggling strings.

"Invincible. I like that." Curled Mustache nodded affirmatively and purposely at the Department of Defense representative, easily identifiable by the sharp suit.

Curled Mustache said, "We need a viable sample of this bacterium in a week. Can you do that?"

Success! I would move mountains with my fist, if that was what it took. "Absolutely."

"Great. Then these are the rest of the dates." Curled Mustache, clearly the director, slid a stack of documents across the table, and I sat to look them over, fingers eager to sign. He tapped the lines as he explained them. "You can see payments are sent with each of the two primary objectives—a smaller one for a viable sample, and a larger one for delivery of the first shipment. If you can meet these deadlines for the product, we can sign right here. If you can't, we'll have to choose another company."

The only possible competition waiting in their wings like a lurking panther ready to strike was Ted Bastion, who I personally nicknamed Ted Bastard. It was fitting.

I grinned reassuringly. "Your search ends here. I'll make those dates, and you can count on that."

Curled Mustache beamed. "Excellent. Let's get this signed, shall we?"

Everything in my entire life hinged on getting these payouts. As Lauren had said, I was broke. Beyond broke, after fronting loans to cover the research and development of this new bacterium. I was going to lose everything if this contract fell through. I hungrily grabbed a pen and said, "Time's ticking."

Curled Mustache chuckled. "I like the way you think."

Maybe when I collected those payments, and Lauren saw those dollar signs, and I took her ring shopping for one that wasn't 'too small' by her standards, she'd finally understand. She'd finally stay. I only needed a little more time.

4

She Speaks

THE KNOCK ON MY elevator door was unexpected, and when I opened the door, a massive spear of hope exploded in me.

"I didn't want to come here, but I felt like I owed you an explanation." The brunette I loved for years was different this time. Less confident. Less swagger. Her clothes were loose, and she wore jeans and sneakers. The change was so remarkable, I couldn't deny her, even if she didn't have a box in her hands.

I wanted her to say she made a mistake. "Is everything okay?"

"Can I come in?"

I moved aside, and Lauren walked in, and after I closed the door, she pushed the box into my hands.

"What's all this...?" I asked while skimming the contents, some of it becoming familiar. "Wait, is this *my* stuff?"

"What did you think it was?" Lauren lifted a brow.

"I thought you changed your mind. You wanted to marry me, and this was you moving in." I never felt more pathetic than at that moment. Not even when I was begging Chris to stop beating me to a pulp. Not when my dad shouted the nastiest things at me, and I ran to my room, crying. Nope. This right here. Thinking this woman genuinely cared about me. This woman who was so different from me that I couldn't figure out what she saw in me in the first place...

...well, I was a very sexy dude.

But I meant otherwise, of course.

"Moving in?" Disbelief shifted her beautiful face. Her makeup, more subdued, wasn't streaked. Her eyes were clear and white. There was no sign of distress on her at all. Lauren sighed. "I thought the dinner was a heart-to-heart about you always being away. That you were going to be home more and give up this company."

Mom and Chris's words thrown back in my face made me grit my teeth.

"I'm here for you, you know that," I said gently.

"When it's convenient for you," she countered. "Your baby is this company, and your favorite dog is that fish tank. I'm not sure where I ranked, but after I saw how small that ring was, I knew it wasn't high enough for me."

I set the box on the table I hadn't bothered to put away yet, and I raked a hand through my layers. Because of her accusation, I deliberately avoided going to my aquarium. Instead, I headed for the door next to it.

My equipment room hummed with energy, running the life-preserving machines which kept a tropical reef thriving high in the sky above the city. Between my fish guy's visits, I frequently checked on the equipment's status, just in case, even though most everything in the room had a redundancy or two built in, protecting the delicate life against power outages and failures.

I heard Lauren follow me in.

"I don't know what to say," I said, bending over the sump and pressing my tie against my chest to protect the material from saltwater damage. The skimmer had been emptied recently. The automatic top-off was functioning as expected—making up for evaporation.

"I tell you this fish tank is more important than me, and the first thing you do is run to your fish tank. Can't you see how wrong that is?"

The RODI water supply was low, which meant something wasn't working correctly. I woke my cell phone and typed a message to my fish guy to check the float switch on his next visit.

"This *is* me," I said, surprised. "And you knew that before. Why is it a problem now? What changed?"

I remembered rolling my suitcase through the gate at the airport like it was yesterday, and the stunning brunette full of smiles and surrounded by people captured my attention. I didn't know who she was, but her ease with people asking invasive questions and snapping photos of her like she was a celebrity or a piece of art had stilled my feet. And when she looked my way, I was lost to her. She'd said, 'Your turn, handsome. Take your pic so I can get out of here.'

I'd said, 'One pic would never be enough.'

Lauren had tilted her head at me, puzzled by my answer and the lack of a camera in my hand. I knew at that moment I had to do whatever it took to woo the princess. So I learned to ski. I gained connections with the big boys. I learned first class was a terrible way to travel. Ha.

I never cared about Lauren's upbringing, honestly, but knowing she had enough to take care of herself reduced the pressure on me to support her and her tastes. Because I was staking my entire future on this company, and I didn't want to drag her down on the chance Dennis was right.

"It means I don't dwell on the past," Lauren said, answering my question as clearly as mud.

I rose and faced her. "Are you saying I do?"

"You're so hung up on your parents you can't see the forest for the trees."

She had no idea what she was talking about, and her assumption had me swallow back an outburst. Calmly, I said, "I only focus on the forest. Remember how you accurately accused me of only loving this building? This is the future. My work here will change lives."

"Your inability to see what is right in front of you is going to make you miserable. This hyper focus on a pipe dream of saving the world is going to destroy you."

The anger flared. "Are you saying I'm going to fail?" Even speaking the word made my blood pressure thrash through my veins.

"I can see their point. I hoped you'd untangle yourself from Mommy's apron strings and do what was best for you...and me. Not trying to prove them wrong all the time."

"Best for us? Who do you think all this is for? I'm working every waking moment to do more with my life, to be more, to earn you a living you deserve. For you."

"If you think any of this is for me...you truly can't see the forest for the trees."

I gave her a fake smile. "Well, I guess you have it all figured out."

Lauren glared at my protein skimmer, bubbling up to lift out dissolved solids. "Good luck with everything. You'll need it."

"I don't want your luck."

"You have no right to be upset with me. I was there for you and supported you. I hoped you would choose right...choose me. Over and over you chose this pile of bricks and those fish. I was second—third class to you, and I was neglected. I came here today, politely, to give you back your things and explain it to you, but you keep throwing it in my face. Your nasty fish reek, and I can't believe you choose them over me." Lauren turned to leave, but she paused by the glass.

"Seriously?"

I followed her. "What?"

"You threw my ring into your fish tank? Wow. I'm surprised. I shouldn't be, but here I am. Baffled. You know what?" Lauren faced me. "Fuck you." She stormed out the door. "I never want to see your face again, if that wasn't clear. Fuck you, Nick."

I blinked for a beat before processing what the hell had just happened. The elevator descended, and I closed the penthouse door behind her. Leaning my back against it, my gaze traveled to the ring I'd tossed into the water.

'Too small' was an excuse. Money wouldn't change her mind. Money wouldn't make her respect me.

After a long day schmoozing figureheads, various corporate stakeholders, and the public, all I needed was my fish. They deserved to swim with their treasure more than Lauren deserved to wear it. They wouldn't insult me.

They wouldn't make demands. They wouldn't interfere with my plans.

I had a contract with critical deadlines, and I couldn't afford any distractions. As much as it hurt, she did me a favor.

5

Small Potatoes

A FEW STORIES BENEATH the parking garage of NBB, down the hall where no one journeyed, I pressed on a discreet panel not much bigger than my hand. What happened down here was secret, as per the confidentiality agreement I'd signed. Besides, I didn't want an opportunist to sell secrets to the media at my expense. So I maintained the strictest controls. Only the secret lab's employees had access, including one housekeeper, but his services were restricted to the lab to minimize risk. And all these employees had an exclusive entrance out of sight from the ones above ground. I wouldn't allow a single one of them access, even Dr. Tyler Gibson, without signing their own ironclad non-disclosure agreement. In total, eight people knew the lab existed.

The square shifted back and glided to the side, exposing a scanner for my palm. I splayed my hand across the screen and waited for the laser to make its pass. I'd had the option to add a retinal scanner, but eyeball stuff freaked me out, so I declined.

The secure door hissed as it opened, releasing negative pressure. I stepped inside the anteroom, and the door closed itself behind me. Antiseptic and lemons filled my nose, and I smiled. Clean. Neat. The way everything should be, which was also why I was a fish guy over dogs and cats.

Especially cats.

Hidden shelving appeared from behind faux walls, allowing access to put on personal protective equipment—booties, face masks, clear plastic face shields, hairnets, and what the geeks affectionately called the bunny suit. I preferred marshmallow suit, but either way, the full-body disposable outfit was white and one-size-fits-most—big, baggy, and universally unflattering. I gowned up.

Since the exterior lab security was so sophisticated, I had to make cuts to finish constructing it. The interior door's security was the same as all the other ordinary doors around the building. I swiped my identification badge through the security slot and the glass doors belched open. Clipping my ID badge to the outside of my marshmallow suit, I stepped inside.

A handful of microbiologists in their clean white suits shuffled around, carrying papers or samples. Rows of stainless-steel counters were speckled with petri dishes, microscopes, computers, and test tubes in glass racks. I hadn't the faintest idea what most of it was for, but whatever my lab manager asked for, I somehow made it happen. Dr. Tyler Gibson agreed to run my lab for the right price, because a man's gotta eat, especially with a young family. I promised him generous bonuses with each completed contract milestone, and after signing those life-changing documents, I knew Dr. Gibson was worth every penny.

I headed toward the doctor, avoiding hyper focused geeks on the way.

"Hey, boss! A cheerful visitor is always welcome down here in the dungeon." Dr. Gibson rose from a stool and closed the distance, hand reaching out to shake. After a tiny hesitation, I shook. I didn't like being in the lab any more than necessary with deadly experimental germs freely walking around. I also understood the irony of choosing pharmaceuticals to satisfy my entrepreneurial itch.

"Gibson." I smiled behind my face mask and clear shield. The mask was scratchy, and the shield was an awkward weight on my head; I didn't envy the workers wearing them all day. "How's the wife?"

My top geek—my affectionate term for the microbiologists and lab technicians for obvious reasons—stood a little shorter than my average five-foot-ten height, and the man glowed thinking of Annie. His smile accented the tilt of his glasses, which he fixed with a practiced scrunch of his nose. "She's so much happier after leaving her last place. She's teaching at the private elementary school instead, and they have a great maternity leave benefit. Oh, here's a funny story. You know how she's wearing an eye patch temporarily? Well, this one student asked her if she's a pirate and if she's going to share the booty." Dr. Gibson laughed. "Kids are great. We can't wait until ours gets here...."

And my brain checked out, so I didn't cringe at Dr. Gibson's story and upset him. Gibson was good people, but tales of kids, their messes, and the noise... All I could hear was shattering glass in my penthouse, and wide, innocent—but guilty—eyes staring at me in extreme regret. Pile on the thought of dirty diapers, and sprinkle in some of Lauren's angry rant, and I had no interest in the fairer sex, distracting me from more important causes.

Sensing Gibson had finished updating me on his private life, I chuckled along with him. "Oh, kids are not for me, but I'm glad everything is going well on the home front."

"Kids are great, but definitely not for everyone." Gibson laughed.

I could hug the guy if it weren't for the deadly bacteria and the potential for contamination. Instead, I changed the subject. "Any progress down here?"

The charts and graphs I'd presented to the CDC were mostly theoretical. The doctor had to make them real.

Dr. Gibson beamed and motioned for me to follow. "This sample is showing great promise. It's been viable in the open air for a full day now, and I consider that a success."

"Music to my ears, Gibson, sweet, sweet music."

"Come, take a look." The microbiologist pressed buttons on a plastic-wrapped remote control, projecting an enlarged image of the current contents under his microscope against a white wall. I didn't know much about the inner workings of bacteria or their resistance to various antibiotics, but even I could tell this enlarged image wasn't normal. It matched the theoretical presentation slides.

I grinned. "Just what the government ordered."

"It is." Dr. Gibson added and smiled, hidden behind a mask, but the wrinkles around the eyes gave it away. "In a few more days, I'll have a full, viable sample to send to Atlanta."

"Excellent. But you know I'm a capitalist, after all. Taking an order and collecting the check due are small potatoes. Someone—some country, or rogue group—somewhere is getting this invincible bacteria."

"Bacterium," the doctor corrected.

"Right. And now...I need the cure."

Dr. Gibson lifted a nearby test tube filled with a red liquid. He swirled it with exaggerated enthusiasm, as if unveiling the newest concept car to a group of thirsty billionaires. "After endless trial and error, this is the only substance on earth that will kill this new bacterium. Why do you want it?"

"Gibson, you're good people, and I don't want to see good people like you get hurt. So when the government orders a lethal new strain of bioweapon for undisclosed purposes, I get a little itchy. The government gets their toy, and we make out like silent thieves in the process, but when the world is begging...or praying...for help in the midst of a panic, I'll be there with the answers. Of course, my services, like yours, aren't free."

Gibson carefully returned the test tube to the rack. "You are one sneaky devil. Congratulations are in order. Those big dreams of yours are about to become reality."

"Thank you, Gibson. Means a lot." Damn, I blinked away tears. My employee was more supportive than my own family.

"I wouldn't want your liability insurance premiums, though." The most brilliant geek in the world laughed.

Through all the planning and organizing, I hadn't put too much thought into insurance—liability, namely. Success had been literally a pipe dream until moments ago. But Gibson had a point. The insurance company didn't know about the contract. And if something catastrophic happened down here, the insurance payout would be grossly insufficient to rebuild and cover all my losses. Gibson's work was critical, and he didn't need extra pressure of knowing just how precarious all this was. "You sure? The insurance company loves me."

"I bet," Gibson smiled.

"Where's the new bacterium being stored?"

Gibson pointed to a clear vault embedded in the wall, lit like a museum display case and just as secure. "It's fully protected against accidents and thieves. Internal controls prevent anyone from tampering with it. Don't worry, boss."

The man was brilliant at his job, and he'd thought of everything down here, but even the doctor had his limits. "Have you named it yet?"

Dr. Gibson lifted a brow. "Hadn't occurred to me. I think you should do the honors."

Not that I'd been thinking about it, but I'd been thinking about it. "The Annihilator sounds fitting, considering without that magical little red tube, it can destroy every human on the planet."

"That was dark." Dr. Gibson blinked and cleared his throat. "We aren't sure *everyone* is susceptible, but we've been labeling it Bacillusly 666 as a joke."

I arched my brows, not catching on.

"It means 'a Bacillus-like bacterium' and it's numbered after the pure evil it is."

Cute. "I like The Annihilator better."

Gibson chuckled. "I do, too. Sounds like a sweet A.O.E. move." Gibson swiped the air, and I was lost all over again. Likely it was something the geeks spoke.

Gibson cleared his throat. "Area of effect?" Still nothing. "Forget it."

I might not speak geek, but the antibiotic needed a name, too. "Any clinically boring name for the antibiotic?"

"Experimental antibiotic for Bacillusly 666 version 47. Tentatively labeled Bacillimycin."

I was afraid to ask what he planned on naming his kids. "That's a mouthful. For the sake of news broadcasters and potentially Chris Barnes's ad copy, how about something punchy...like *Heromycin*?"

Gibson grimaced. "A little on the nose, don't you think?"

"Only a hero can destroy the ultimate evil we created. It needs to have a memorable name. Bonus points if it's easily spoken and spelled, and since it's clear from the name what it does, it's marketing gold." The geek just squinted. "We're riding the wrong wavelengths here. Trust me. This is Chris's area, and I've argued with him enough to have picked up a few things."

"I trust you, boss." Something beeped, catching Gibson's attention briefly. "Well, the deadline is coming, and I have work to do."

I could kiss the man. "I see you have everything under control around here, so I won't waste any more of your time."

"Actually, I do have one problem," Gibson said.

"Fixing problems is what I do. Lay it on me." I'd gotten this far. Anything else was a lump in the gravy.

"I have only a handful of staff. I know it's to minimize risk—the fewer people aware, the better. I get it. But if I'm going to make the required quantity by the date schedule, I need more staff. That first shipment is going to be tough to meet, if not nearly impossible."

Minor problems were a pleasant diversion from the harder ones. I gave my friend a reassuring smile hidden behind my mask. "More small potatoes. I'll take care of it. Let me know if you need anything else."

"Can do. Later, boss." Gibson dropped onto his stool and squinted into the microscope.

I returned to the anteroom and hastily peeled off my disposable protective equipment, happy to be free of that scratchy polyester. I stuffed the wad down the chute and straightened my tie. With the press of my hand against a screen, I strolled out on a mission for more employees. Piece of cake.

Huh. After Dennis kicked me out from Thanksgiving Birthday, I missed out on cake. I kind of wanted some.

6

A Bet

I WAS ON TOP of the world. Not literally, but since I lived on the twentieth floor of a cutting-edge pharmaceutical company in one of the greatest cities in the USA, I might as well have been. I whistled as I headed to my favorite manager's floor when a giggling conversation stopped me short, and I listened.

My perky young assistant, Chelsea, was currently cleaning up the mobile coffee station after a meeting. But that wasn't all she was doing.

"Did she really say that?" Chelsea asked.

I was good with faces and names, and I only needed a moment to recall who this chatty woman next to her was—Analeigh, a buyer in the purchasing department. The blond nodded enthusiastically, and I leaned back so I wouldn't be spotted. "What kind of manager would say something like that? I couldn't believe it. Honestly, I'm surprised she's still here."

"Purchasing managers are hard to find, especially when dealing with raw materials from overseas. The language barrier alone is tough," my lovely assistant said. She was too brilliant for that position, but her resume had been all desk jobs—not a geek background anywhere.

Shame.

"I suppose," Analeigh said. "So if I'm amazing at my job, I can slack off with the intention of getting fired to collect unemployment?"

"It doesn't work that way." Chelsea wrapped the remaining stack of cups. "If you get fired for cause, you won't qualify, but if you were laid off through no fault of your own, then you do. If Heather's admitting she's only here because her family needs her to be, she's doing it wrong."

My brows rose. What an interesting but incredibly convenient development.

"No kidding. I'll see you at lunch, Chelsea." Analeigh waved and left, carrying her cup of brew, and Chelsea pushed the coffee cart away.

A problem just solved itself. I whistled while I took the elevator to the next floor down, wove through the cubicles, and strolled past the glass-fronted offices to find Heather Brush, feet up on her desk, and Andras File next to her. My Chief Information Officer and close friend...er, only friend, strained the seams of his suit as he hunched over the dwarfed desk. When we hit the gym together, one floor beneath my penthouse, Andras demolished me on the power rack, and because of the man's lumbering size, he was a fun boxing opponent—not afraid to take hits. Andras claimed the trick to his shredded frame was balancing macros. Many people didn't want to admit they juiced, and even though I didn't appreciate lying, that fib was okay by me, because it hurt no one but himself.

I gave a polite knock on the door, and when the pair turned to look at me, they straightened immediately. I never expected Andras to have a thing for Heather, an early-thirties woman, who wore a well-fitted suit coat matching her pencil skirt. Her black hair was pulled back into a serious bun, and her thin lips were swiped with bright red lipstick. She came across as business-minded and tough, which was why I'd hired her to make sure our critical orders arrived on time. But her performance had been sliding lately, which I'd noticed and could correct, but since her subordinates knew she deliberately slacked in her duties, this situation needed more than a correction.

Heather waved me inside as Andras straightened and innocently adjusted his cuffs. "Hey, boss, I was just headed up to see you."

"Mind if I have a chat with Heather for a minute?" I didn't want to toss my friend out, but I figured she'd want privacy for this delicate matter.

"Can he stay?" Heather asked and glanced at Andras.

Heather didn't seem like the type to need a support system, but I tried not to get too personal with my employees, for reasons beginning with this one. "In that case, I have a problem to fix, and I think you're the right person for the job."

Heather sat up formally. "Is that so?"

"How long have you worked here?" I kept my tone light and friendly. No need to worry her.

"One year, three months, and six days."

I tilted my head at her, completely not expecting such a detailed count, as if she dreaded each and every day. I chuckled. "Are you sure?"

Heather shared another glance with Andras, and said, "I like to keep track of milestones."

I rested my palms on the backrest of the empty chair in front of her desk. "Well, I'm a big believer in efficiency, and today I intend to solve two problems at once."

Heather grinned nervously.

"I hear you'd rather be laid off and collect unemployment than show up here to run my purchasing department. I have to admit, when I heard this, I was taken aback. We are saving lives here, and I pay everyone well. Is this rumor true? Would you rather sit at home than be part of something this great?"

Heather's face flushed bright red. She met Andras's gaze once more, and he shrugged. "No, I'd...rather be here," she said slowly.

"See, this is where my problem comes in. I need to hire geeks, and since you don't want to be here, and your salary would cover a couple, I don't need you anymore."

"But someone still has to do my job," Heather protested. "You're just shuffling people around, and I already know what I'm doing."

She had a point. "I need to make budgetary cuts to your department. Can you think of any assets that can be spared?"

"I'm not sure." Heather glanced around her office as if looking for something to sell. Everyone specialized in this company, but a thorough knowledge of one's entire department workflows was important.

"While you take the time to think through a process improvement, I'll point out a few areas of concern: customs delaying the import of raw materials, a continuous rolling schedule of shortages, expedited processing and shipping charges for last-minute orders. Anything here you could work with?"

Heather smiled. "If the production manager scheduled the work-in-progress better, my ordering team could foresee orders better and reduce the expedited order fees."

That was something. "Great! How much would that save from your budget?"

"Oh, maybe five hundred dollars a month?" With the lilt of her voice, she only guessed.

"You don't know?"

"Not off the top of my head. Do you think I pour over numbers and analyze every invoice or catalog every complai...nt." She dragged out the last word as she focused on my face.

"Heather, you're fired."

Her mouth gaped open like a fish, and she rose. Her gaze returned to Andras briefly, as if pleading for backup. "You can't do that to me!"

Andras let out a quiet chuckle. "He just did."

Heather darted daggers at him. "What's so funny?"

Andras laughed. "I'm sorry, it's just. Sorry."

"I can't believe this," Heather said, voice rising. People beyond the glass were looking our way. "You can't do this to me. I've been here a year, three months, and six days. I was almost done!" The purchasing manager collected an armful of personal items, steaming from the hair down to the heels. Gawkers filled the glass, not even trying to be discreet about it.

"It's not personal, Heather. Please don't make a scene," I said.

"A scene? You don't want *me* to make a scene?" Heather's voice kept rising.

Andras chuckled again.

"You asshole!" she shouted at Andras, and he covered his face with a broad palm, shoulders bouncing. If he hoped to get up her skirt, that wasn't happening now. I bit back my own amusement as Heather stomped out the door and pushed her way through the gawkers.

"That went well," I said.

Andras laughed.

"What is so funny?"

"It's nothing." Andras swatted the air. "It's just... We had a bet she wouldn't make it a year and a half here, and she lost. Heather doesn't like to lose."

"That I believe. What were the stakes?" I couldn't help but ask. It was such a bizarre thing to wager against.

"Something she hates more than anything." Andras wasn't going to elaborate, but that was fine. Heather wouldn't be in my life any longer, anyhow.

"Join me in the gym tonight?"

"Of course."

7

Therapeutic

As weird as Heather's outburst was over being fired and losing a bet at the same time, she had been right about one thing. She might be gone, but someone had to fill her spot. I didn't have a net gain of cash to use for hiring. If one could not cut expenses, then increasing income was the next best thing.

I reluctantly headed to my brother's office. Since the big family blowout during our annual Thanksgiving Birthday meal, Chris avoided me entirely, and I was fine with that, but he still had to do his job to keep it. Although, I would love nothing more than to fire him out of spite.

His door was open, but I knocked out of courtesy.

Chris frowned but said nothing.

"Can I have a word?" I asked after the awkward silent beat.

He gestured in the affirmative. "What's up?" Chris said, not at all enthusiastic about seeing my handsome mug.

"I have a small problem, and I need to increase sales to fix it."

Chris blinked. "That's what you have to say to me?"

So he wanted to dredge up the past. "As far as I understood what transpired, I am no longer part of the family. You're here for a job, nothing more, so I have nothing to say about it."

Chris snorted derisively. "Just like you, Nick."

I didn't want my mission to be derailed for anything, especially not his petty drama. "Are you refusing to do your job?"

Chris pressed his lips thin. "More ads."

I needed detail. I sat on the edge of his desk, stacked neatly with portfolios of campaigns to be approved or declined. But he didn't comment on my intrusion. "Care to elaborate on *how* Marketing expects to leverage more ads to boost sales?"

Chris's face burned red, very similar to Dennis's when he was in a mood. When Chris and I had fought as children and teens, Chris always turned a funny shade of red. The next day, the telltale bruises darkened his skin. A long time had passed since we'd tumbled for any reason, but after that ridiculous dinner full of insults, the urge to serve the man a fist sandwich was overwhelming. My brother and I never saw eye to eye on anything.

"Push the drug reps to focus on the universal aspect of Anycillin and design new pamphlets to showcase this." Rather than give the usual answer I was expecting—design a witty campaign, film it, and buy air space—Chris pushed the responsibility onto another department entirely. That was low, even for him.

And his solution? Pamphlets. A multi-million-dollar company offering world-class antibiotics with drug representatives traveling from coast to coast, convincing providers to choose Anycillin over our competitors...and Chris wanted to splash color on some paper.

"Hit the providers from both sides," Chris continued with a sparking idea, and his voice grew with excitement. "New TV ads pushing consumers to demand what they need at the doctor's offices, and the drug reps pushing the providers to choose ours over the competition. I have an idea for a great television ad. First, we start with happy families..."

Chris knew nothing about the concept. Holiday gatherings were always a ticking time bomb. If it wasn't something Uncle Bert said to Cyndi, then it was something inappropriate Dennis said to Aunt Sally. Then Chris would defend his wife, and somehow my name would be slung around while World War III descended the Barnes's household. If I'd kept numerical track, the digits would be far too long, so I'd always referred to each incident as World War III.

No soldier stood down until the food was served. If it was an unusually polite fight, everyone scattered shortly after clearing their plates. If not, the police broke up the festivities—similar to Stella and Chris's Thanksgiving Birthday dinner, only louder and with more broken glass. Sometimes blood. Mom didn't get her eclectic mix of dinnerware because of her taste in style. And since Dennis had banned me from the house, I had the perfect excuse to skip it from now on, a gift that kept on giving.

When he finished, I said, "I have a different idea, Chris. Happy families can advertise anything from ketchup to real estate. NBB needs to be more daring, more memorable than that." I rose and paced the tight office. "How about we downplay the danger of germs?"

Chris's pudgy face twisted with disgust. "I'd love to hear this from *you.*"

Ignoring that jab, I said, "People love parties, family gatherings, and vacations, but these things are limited during cold and flu season. If people aren't afraid of germs at all, they'll be more willing to gather, which makes them happier. Following?"

"Unfortunately."

I ignored that too. "And *when* they get sick, NBB's Anycillin will make the aches go away—the quick fix to feel better. Increasing demand will increase revenues."

"Our antibiotic doesn't work on viruses," Chris countered.

"We're under no obligation to explain," I said.

"And that will add to the antibiotic overuse problem," Chris said.

"It's not overuse if they think they need it," I said with a smart grin. I dragged my palms across the air in the shape of a rainbow and recited the company slogan. "NBB Pharmaceuticals—Feel Better, One Cure at a Time."

Chris stood. "You think it's a great idea to increase demand for our products by making people reckless with their health?"

I didn't appreciate my tactics being questioned. "Please, do give me a better idea."

Chris sighed. "Would you really sink that low? Manipulating people with unethical information is a new one, even for you."

"There's nothing unethical about making promises a company can keep. If customers are told family is more important than worrying about sickness, which is true, and NBB can cure them, which is also true, there is no ethical conundrum here."

"Being safe with one's health is more important than family barbecues or Thanksgivings." He pointedly paused. With that example, I agreed. "Nick, just because you can, doesn't mean you should."

And that was one reason why Chris job-hopped for years—insubordination, because of his holier-than-thou beliefs—but before I could get a word in, which would escalate the argument, Chris approached and added, "There's something else I need to mention."

A cat hair on his sport coat swayed with his movements, twitching my eye.

"Kelly mentioned, and I noticed—"

"Who?" I interrupted. I made a point of learning everyone's name, but that one eluded me. I continued to glare at the rogue blemish, fingers itching to pull it off.

"Don't you even," Chris warned.

Unable to help myself, I pressed my lips thin with disgust and pulled the wayward hair. I released it over the trash.

Chris swatted his sport coat as if brushing away my touch. "Kelly is the new human resources manager. She said the turnover in this company is higher than the industry benchmark. Maybe you should offer a gesture of appreciation to the employees."

At first, I was impressed at his ability to be helpful by spotting areas of improvement. "Schedule the entire building for a mental health webinar." Another problem solved.

"That's not good enough. I was thinking a little something to soften the unease around here."

"What do you mean?"

"Well," Chris spoke carefully. "You always talk about lowering costs. High employee turnover is expensive. Something cheap, like a gift card or a cash bonus, would show everyone you're not..." Chris trailed off.

What could've been an astute suggestion became additional expenses, with a trailed off insult. Chris was a chip off the old Dennis block, just less bold, but only because I was in a position of authority. Back in the day, Chris wouldn't have held back.

"That's enough."

"It wouldn't hurt you to stop being an asshole sometimes," Chris added.

My jaw clenched, and I glared at my brother. I wasn't an asshole. I was just...tenacious and ambitious, and I could see the bigger picture—*eat your heart out, Lauren*. I said slowly, "Everyone around here should be thankful for a job." My threat was directed at my idiot older brother.

The red seeped up Chris's face, telling me loud and clear he understood. "You've reached the top of your own world and have everything you ever wanted, but somehow that stick is still up your ass."

I barely refrained from hitting the man, since grown adults controlled themselves, but I was being tested here. "For the record, you have no idea what I want. You were always too busy getting everything you wanted...at my expense." Eh, sometimes the past needed to be dredged, and now I was feeling petty.

"You're never going to change, are you?"

I snorted derisively. Without Mom interfering, I could finally say what I wanted. "I'm helping people. I'm curing people. I'm saving lives, and with all of that said, I can't see how you're blind to it. Someone has to do my job, and if having a stick up my ass—whatever that means—is necessary, then yes, call me Vlad's new best friend."

Chris's eyelid twitched, but I wasn't done yet. What I wanted to do was fire him. I wanted to so badly I could taste it, but since I needed revenues to increase, begrudgingly, I probably needed Chris. "Now, if you want to keep your job, I suggest you add value around here."

Chris slapped his laptop closed. "I'm taking lunch." He barreled out the door with a constipated look on his face. I was working on changing the world, and Chris didn't even care.

Today didn't get me the immediate results I needed, but it was sure therapeutic. I leaned over Chris's desk and dialed down to Kelly, the new human resources manager. She answered immediately, so I already liked her.

"This is Kelly."

"Kelly, Nick Barnes here. Listen, I have an opening for a purchasing department manager. Change the pay range down twenty percent. With that savings, I need you to find me a geek."

"A what?" she asked.

Kelly was new. "A lab technician, and they'll report directly to me."

"I can do that," she said simply.

Good girl. "Thank you."

Therapeutic and a little successful. Not a bad day at all.

8

Hallucination

As much as today felt like a win, I had pent-up energy to burn, so I was grateful Andras and I had a date at my private gym. The scent of rubber and cleaning supplies always calmed me. I added ten miles under my belt while the swish of the hoops, squeaks of the sneakers, and cheers of the crowd kept my mind busy. I mopped the sweat from my brow, keeping a close eye on the NBA finals.

The treadmill beeped and came to a careful stop. Panting, I uncapped my water bottle, squirted a mouthful, swished, and swallowed. The door to the gym clattered open. I glanced in one of the numerous mirrors lining the walls. Andras lumbered in, wearing appropriate workout shorts and a tank with a white towel draped around the nape of his neck and a bottle of water in his enormous hand.

"Here, I thought you weren't going to make it tonight."

"It was a close one." Andras flashed his perfect whites and sat on the rower, draping his arms across the handlebars. "I found some information you'll be interested in."

I didn't normally want to discuss work after hours, but since I still didn't have what Dr. Tyler Gibson needed, I said, "I'm all ears." I toweled the sweat off my arms and neck and cheers echoed through the gym. I glanced at the game briefly and sat on the treadmill belt, eyes level with my friend.

"I was working with Jason Flick to audit a few areas." Jason was my accounting manager, a nervous squirrely man, but he knew his stuff. "That's why I was in Heather's office. After I searched the wholesale order histories, one particular wholesaler dramatically reduced its order volume."

That was mixed news—good to have a lead to chase, but bad for revenues. "And you discovered a reason?"

"No, and I didn't get a chance to ask Heather for her thoughts since you fired her. I can schedule a deep dive on it later this week."

And that was a man capable of getting things done. "I knew I liked you."

Andras chuckled. "Well, you may not like this next part. The miscellaneous expense line, the one you insist on fully controlling, is far beyond industry standard. I don't understand why, but it needs to be addressed."

In an attempt to keep my perilous project—now confirmed contract—safe, all daily expenses for it, including payroll, electricity, and supplies, were handled through the miscellaneous expense on the profit-and-loss statement. I personally accounted for each expense to Jason Flick. If audited, everything was above board, but he, like Andras, didn't know the details of what those expenses were for.

"I'll take it into consideration," I said dismissively. Not only would I not cut anything from Dr. Gibson's lab, but I needed to increase his allowance.

"Can I ask you something?" Andras shifted on the rower, as if his body size didn't comfortably fit the seat.

"Go ahead." And I'd answer, as long as it didn't involve my secret lab.

"Several years ago, there was this friend of mine. Call her...Gertie. She was a lovely lady, truly, but through no fault of her own, Gertie's family disowned her, and she already didn't have many friends. Gertie lost her support system, and the trauma associated with losing her family steered her wrong. Eventually, I noticed her dark path."

I swigged water from my bottle, unable to help noticing a coincidental parallel here. This was a beating-around-the-bush way of warning me about something, but I didn't take orders from people. Andras knew that.

"Gertie was special to me."

Okay, maybe I was wrong. Maybe Andras had a dear friend with a similar background to me. I'd never heard him mention his love life, and although I hated when people—namely, my family—prodded into my personal life, I couldn't help my curiosity. Since Andras was offering, I asked, "Did you date her?"

Andras chuckled. "Me? No, not at all. It wasn't like that. Many people could see she was headed for a grave mistake, so she was given an irresistible offer to change course. It would've meant an easy and fun life, and Gertie wouldn't have had to interact with humans directly again, if she preferred."

Andras's use of 'humans' for a descriptor was unusual, and this whole thing was ridiculous. "I'm missing something. If her offer was to never interact with humans again, was she offered a ticket to Mars? Is that it? The solution to her problem was to leave the planet. What is the point of this?"

"Wrong direction," Andras said simply.

We were back in fairy tale land. I said dryly, "The suspense is killing me."

"Then you'll love this part. Gertie turned down the offer. She actually declined to have a fun and easy life. If you want to know, yes, she lived miserably ever after. The end."

I couldn't say I'd take a trip to Mars in the wrong direction, either. "She didn't change her mind later?"

"Oh, she did, but the offer was gone by then. Her stubbornness led to her misery."

"I don't get the relevance."

Andras leaned in closer. "Would you have taken the deal—if you were Gertie?"

I shook my head. "Good thing you're not in sales. I'd need way more information to make any kind of judgment call."

My friend laughed and removed the towel from his neck. Andras slung it over the armrest of the stair-stepper next to him and said, "What if this was about a partnership?"

Finally, we reached the punchline. I laughed, but Andras only waited with a calm face. "You're serious?"

"A partnership that will lead to a fun and easy life. It's not a joke."

"One so great that Gertie turned it down? Look, I'm the last guy on this planet who'd take on a partner. Against vitriol and belittling criticism, I built a successful company by myself." I hated the resistance my family had given me, and my face scrunched with memories I wished I could forget. "Although I did have an understanding loan officer. After NBB opened doors, I sent him a fruit basket. Good ol' Chuck Leach."

Andras's eyes glowed like a pair of red rubies in the sunlight or a pair of red flashlights in the dark of night. They were stunningly beautiful, but also completely terrifying. I stilled. There had to be a reasonable explanation. I replayed all my memories of Andras, trying to decide if the man had only been a figment of my imagination, like Odie, the frustrating elephant. Andras definitely interacted with Heather, and he was working with Jason Flick. So he had to be real. My pulse quickened.

Brain tumor.

THE ONLY EXPLANATION WAS I had a brain tumor, but I was too young to die. I had too much to accomplish. I checked my watch to see if the clinic was still open. It was not. Just great. My parents would probably dance on my grave...after my mom's crocodile tears dried. But Lauren... By pure luck she'd turned down my proposal—sparing herself worse pain later. Maybe instinct told her I was a dead end. I blinked. I couldn't die now. Everything I busted my Vlad-friendly ass for was ultimately for nothing. That was damned depressing.

I blinked again, but Andras's brown eyes watched me.

A god damned brain tumor. A ball of shitty cells was going to take me down.

"Everything okay?"

Andras was an employee, but he was a friend too, and I was comfortable talking about it. "Don't take this the wrong way, but is something wrong with your eyes? Maybe it's me, and it probably is. My day's been too long, but I swear they...I don't know...glowed." As soon as the word popped out of my mouth, I realized I was an idiot. "You know what? Never mind. That's crazy. I'm under a lot of stress, and now I'm hallucinating."

Too much stress—had to be it, but I didn't *feel* overly stressed. The contract had been secured, and with Heather's departure, there were funds to hire a geek. I didn't have an explanation for the red glowing eyes on Andras.

"Sometimes I get a strange reaction to the fluorescent lights. It's not you." The big man's cold tone was concerning, but so was the disappointment flattening his face.

"What is it, Andras?"

"I know my story sounded strange, but think about it. Can you do me that much?"

"My refusal to partner up isn't personal. It's just—" I couldn't share the glory—that was the asshole hidden down below. Chris could see right through to it.

"I'm a big guy." Andras softened. "No need to sugarcoat it for me. I'm here to help you succeed. You play a bigger part in keeping the world safe than you realize."

That was a pretty nice stroke to the ego. "Curious, not that I'm committing to anything, but what kind of partnership did Gertie turn down?"

Andras beamed. "I have a friend—not Gertie—who has the ability to grant people power. His name is Corson."

"What kind of partnership can guarantee something like that? My contacts in government or the Swiss alps can't do that much."

"It's not a partnership in the traditional business sense. In exchange for receiving the power, you'll have to agree to a specific set of rules and a commitment to assist Corson."

"So, it's not compensated?" I had too many bills. That wasn't going to fly.

"Money won't be an issue."

Apparently, on this trip to Mars in the wrong direction, money was no object. I pinched the bridge of my nose. "Let me see if I'm getting this right. This Corson fellow, who doesn't have the balls to come to me himself, wants me to commit to him, follow his rules, and do who-knows-what for who-knows-how-long in exchange for more power that I don't need and no money? Salesman, you are not." I waved my hand, brushing away the idea. This sounded organized-crime shady, and if Andras File was involved with the mafia, I wouldn't be surprised, but I wanted nothing to do with it.

I continued, "So here's a pointer: If this was how the deal was proposed to Gertie, I don't blame her for turning it down, no matter the miserable consequences. And like her, I have to decline again. I trust my own strength and skills, but please give your friend my apologies. You understand, a man in my position gets here not by taking orders, but by giving them."

Andras leaned on his elbows. Neither one of us was getting much of a workout tonight. "The offer stands whenever you feel compelled."

I swallowed generous gulps from my water bottle and moved into the proper position on the rower next to Andras. I rowed and watched the game, and Andras fell into a rhythm with me, but the possibilities churned. If I had more power, would my reputation draw the best geeks to work for me...at a lower cost? Instead of always paddling upstream alone in this endeavor, having a partner, someone to confide in, like this Corson fellow, meant someone else took a paddle.

Stupid idea. I was an excellent business owner—regardless of Dennis's baseless rants about my continued failure. I didn't need help, and I certainly didn't do partnerships, and there was nothing that could change my mind. Still, curiosity's claws hung steadily.

Since I warmed up with a ten-mile run beforehand, I quit rowing first, and Andras finished shortly thereafter. Both of us faced each other, mopping our faces. I panted from the exertion, but Andras didn't. Just as his deal seemed shady, so did whatever juice he used.

I rose, and Andras followed suit. With the noise of the post-game analysis on the TV, we walked toward the door.

"Is it worth it? I mean, truly, friend to friend here."

Andras gave me a small lift of his lips. "I wouldn't lie to you, and I wouldn't lead you into something that wouldn't benefit you. With that in mind, it's absolutely worth it. I'll see you tomorrow."

"Good night."

What if I could take the deal and walk away when I didn't like it any longer? It wasn't like I had to sign a contract in blood or anything.

9

Medium Potatoes

I SPENT HALF THE morning glancing at the eyes of all the employees passing by my office. I also gazed at inanimate objects, waiting for random visual disturbances to appear, but the strangeness of Andras's glowing red eyes hadn't occurred again, so he was probably right about the odd reflection from the lighting. For now, I decided against scheduling an MRI.

Instead, I checked my encrypted email, and I sucked in a breath.

Dear Mr. Nick Barnes,   We want to inform you that we at the Centers for Disease Control and Prevention have received a delivery from you. The safety of our staff is our first priority, so you'll understand that unpacking and securing the contents took time. We want to thank you, on behalf of our staff and the public at large, for securely packaging the delivery with the utmost care. The package has undergone an initial examination and is found to be satisfactory. On these terms, the contract as signed is now enforceable. We expect the first shipment to be as equally well-packaged and received on time. Payment will be wired upon successful receipt.   It's been a pleasure doing business with you, Mr. Barnes, and we look forward to a successful future with you.   Sincerely,

Drs. Branston and Rhee Centers for Disease Control and Preventionundefined

Since these matters couldn't be discussed in the open, I headed down to see Dr. Tyler Gibson at once, and I found him where he always was, with his masked and shielded face pressed against a microscope.

"Hey, Gibson."

The doctor straightened. "Nick! Any word from Atlanta?"

"They received it, but now the first shipment has to be out the door in two weeks. I promised the CDC and the Department of Defense I could meet their target quantity. Tell me you have good news on that front. Does this green stuff multiply faster than rabbits?"

Gibson chuckled. "From our studies so far, almost. I hate to do this to you, knowing you struggled to get one person in this door who's not trained yet, but we're handling extremely hazardous materials. If we rush, someone is going to break one. I don't know the full airborne capabilities of The Annihilator yet, but we can't take that chance. I can't stress enough how critical having a sufficient team down here is."

"How many people do you need?"

"Honestly?" Gibson scratched the back of his neck. "I want a dozen, but I know that's hard. Space down here is limited, too, but these deadlines..."

A dozen more people. Damn it. This qualified as medium potatoes, and I didn't like it. "I'll do whatever it takes, as always. Your health is my priority."

"Thank you, boss. You're doing good. This is the right thing."

I always liked Gibson. He was good people through and through. I would kick the world's ass for him. But I'd start with wrangling up a dozen more geeks.

Somehow.

I ENDED THE VIDEO conference call with a fresh wave of frustration. Orders of my flagship product, Anycillin, kept this company operating. And the only way I could get my antibiotic into the hands of sick customers was through a distribution channel of wholesalers. One of my most reliable wholesalers claimed NBB's latest delivery was short, and if the order wasn't fulfilled in full by next week, Anycillin was going on the backorder list. I assured him the drugs would be on a truck by nightfall, and I made a few calls. There was a staffing issue from sickness, but if I approved overtime, they could get it done. So I did. More medium potatoes. I'd handled worse before, but the timing sucked.

My interoffice phone rang, and I picked up the call from the accounting department's extension. "Talk to me, Jason."

"Hi, boss. I found an anomaly. The inventory count on cellulose is astronomically higher than normal. Like off the charts."

That was useful. "Do you know why, and if it can be rectified?"

The sound of keys clicking came through the receiver. "The lead purchasing agent said Heather Brush authorized a bulk shipment, because cellulose was rumored to be going on backorder."

That sounded reasonable. "Did it?"

"Apparently, it didn't."

"Can it be returned?"

More clicking came through. "According to the invoice, we're too late for a return authorization."

Of course. I sighed. "Have the name of the supplier in my inbox within the hour. We can't have product spoiling."

I pictured pallets of raw materials in boxes sitting in the warehouse with mice chewing holes through them and defecating all over. Those creepy creatures with scaly tails and little whiskers fluttering in the air freaked me out more than eyeball stuff, and even more than cats, if that were possible. What were they trying to sense, anyway? I'd been curious about the answer, but not enough to research online, risking beady little eyes popping up on my screen. I shivered.

Jason Flick said, "I contacted Production, and she says they'll use all of it."

My eyebrows lifted. "Before it expires?"

"She didn't specify, but I assume so."

"Don't assume. Get facts. Do you have the end-of-quarter figures for me?" A rustling of paper and mumbles carried through the earpiece. "Jason?"

"Uh, yeah, hang on. Here we go." Jason cleared his throat. "Quarter-end profit was lower than Levens projected."

Gary Levens was my headstrong manager of finance, who, so far, accurately predicted future revenues based on historical data. I had no reason to doubt we'd have enough profit this quarter. Less profit meant less money for what really mattered.

"Thanks, Flick."

If I hadn't already fired Heather Brush, I would now. Why didn't anyone else care about the funding for my...*secret*...project? I exhaled. They couldn't stress about it because they didn't know about it, and my inability to disclose it frustrated me even more. If profits for the last quarter were lower than we'd budgeted for, more cuts were needed, and I'd have to defend not only maintaining, but increasing my miscellaneous expense account.

Well, if they didn't like what I did with my company, I'd show them the door. Chris's warning about high employee turnover costing more than the industry standard repeated in my head. I groaned, and a knock on my door had me smoothing my tie. "Come in."

Chris barreled inside with a laptop under his arm. "Don't pick the fuzz off the rug for me. Er, wait. You don't have any fuzz in here."

My appreciation for neat and clean spaces wasn't a defect. While I stared daggers at his pudgy back, Chris placed the laptop on the small, round conference table near my desk. Apparently, my big brother had cooled off. That he appeared to not only be focusing on his job but taking initiative had me curious.

Chris set a stack of documents on the table and connected the laptop to the presentation screen mounted on the wall. His face was lit with an excitement I hadn't seen in a while.

I leaned forward to see the screen better. "What do you have for me?"

Chris sifted through computer applications to find the correct one. "Things were heated the other day, but you were right—we need more than pamphlets to make a noticeable change in the profit needle. This is a storyboard for a brand-new marketing campaign. Everything's ready to go. I just need your stamp of approval to call in the camera crew."

That was the most mature thing Chris had done in a while, and that Chris had actually gone above and beyond impressed me. A lot.

The first digital pencil sketch filled the screen, and he narrated. "The message we're portraying is NBB Pharmaceuticals will protect your family when the competition fails you. We open with an average suburban family with a newborn. Mom finishes slicing raw meat and washes her hands."

Chris clicked to change the image. "Here we zoom in on her hands microscopically, showing the soap she used wasn't good enough. Then Mom coughs in her hands, but Mom is careful. With cold and flu season in full swing, she rubs her hands with a squirt of hand sanitizer. Once again, we zoom, but we see too many germs remain. Mom picks up her giggling newborn, and they play cute infant games. Giggles ensue, and we zoom in again."

I shifted in my seat. A nightmare unfurled on the screen. Although the urge for a shower was strong, I opened my desk drawer and used two pumps of my own hand sanitizer.

Chris's attention shifted to my movements, and my big brother smirked, but he continued without comment. "The germs are now on the baby, and watch here—oh, silly baby's hands go in her mouth! Now we zoom to an animation of cartoon germs flooding the baby's system, but Anycillin splits off into cartoon soldiers, destroying the infection. Cut back to our happy family and the tagline: *Anycillin anytime*. Then we have the narrator speed read the disclaimer."

Although grossly uncomfortable, I was impressed. "You downplayed the danger of germs."

"I did, with a happy family, too, but they aren't reckless. The mom doubles her safety, but it's still not good enough. Instead of blaming the people, we're subliminally blaming other companies."

Taking my brother seriously, I crossed to the table and sat next to him. Colorful charts, columns of numbers, and projected completion dates—Chris had prepared the whole campaign, as he said. "Show me the details."

Before pointing to the cost, Chris said, "This campaign will increase demand at doctor's offices, urgent cares, and emergency rooms. With minor adjustments for cultural differences, this ad campaign will be viable globally, making Anycillin a household name everywhere."

I cleared my throat and blinked back the shimmer in my eye. "That sounds great. What's the damage to run it?"

Chris shifted papers and pointed to the bottom column. "I designed this project to maximize the revenue impact, so...I didn't actually use a budget."

I raked a hand through my styled locks and leaned back. I was convinced by the quality of the work, but

I didn't have the funds in any department's budget. I didn't have personal funds to throw at it, either. Even if I had assets to finance this campaign, and it succeeded, then Christopher P. Barnes would forever take the credit of turning NBB into a global household name. *It means you're a failure, you ungrateful, stubborn bastard.* I couldn't hand the torch of success to my brother, not after all the blood, sweat, and tears I'd invested in starting this company.

I had one option left. The man had pulled through for me before. "Give me until tomorrow to decide."

Chris's prideful smile slid away. He immediately collected his paperwork, tapping it extra forcefully, and unplugged his laptop with an unnecessary yank. "If the answer's no, I'd appreciate you being upfront about it."

"I gave you my answer."

"The famous words from the famous leader." Chris shuffled out of the office without any pleasantries and slammed the door shut behind him.

After all this time, I should be used to disappointment by now, but that wasn't the case. Each flare-up was a fresh slap in the face, a fresh reminder from Dennis about my failures.

Not today, old man.

I turned off the television screen and returned to my desk. As I did for the CDC and the DoD, I assembled my own presentation. Our relationship went way back, so this should be a quick in-and-out. The additional debt would suck, but I'd do it for Chris. I kind of hated him, but I believed in him.

IO

Old Friends

CHUCK LEACH WAS A humorless old man with bushy brows above wire-rimmed glasses. The top of his head reflected the light instead of his youth, but with that age came wisdom and trust. And I was fully confident our lengthy history meant my colorful charts and lists of numbers were simply a formality.

Chuck clicked his pen repeatedly while pursing his lips at the documents I had given him—paper copies of my presentation. On the other side of the desk, I stood next to the screen, eagerly awaiting his first impression. I'd worked on this presentation into the night, skipping dinner, and my stomach growled at the delicious scent of spicy chicken wafting through Chuck's private office at Stars National Bank.

This should be quick.

The desk between us was stacked high with overstuffed folders. The stack on the right corner was three folders higher than the left stack. And the stack to the center-left had several more folders than the other two combined, but they were much thinner, making that stack shorter. The papers were tossed in without care, corners jutting out at random. Trying to focus on the banker, my eye twitched.

With a deep, slow sigh, Chuck Leach flipped pages, pushing out and pulling in his lips as if the repetitive movements helped him concentrate.

My first ever business loan had been approved by Chuck Leach back when the stacks of folders were much lower, and I had been a fresh-faced go-getter. After receiving the approval, I'd told my parents about my plan to buy a defunct and hollowed out drug company. Dennis called me several unflattering descriptors while my mom cried. At the time, I believed Mom was upset about the insult-slinging fight, but after a conversation to 'straighten him out', they were more concerned about the financial burden and the downward spiral I was riding. They weren't chipping in or assisting in any way, and to this day, they never had. Why did they even care at all? Apparently, my determination to make the world a safer place was wasting my life.

But becoming a plumber was worthy of a trophy...of some sort.

My college buddies were more supportive, but none were brave enough to cosign or join my startup ranks. I harbored no ill will against them. I'd rather pay interest to an independent third party than owe part of my livelihood to people with unclear motivations.

Even though my first business did not succeed, as Dennis enjoyed reminding me, Chuck was the man who'd given me a second chance. Because of him, NBB stood tall among its peers, and I knew full well I'd be nothing without Chuck's confidence and trust. So, I refrained from insulting the man by rearranging his documents.

But I really, really wanted to.

The pen clicking stopped, and Chuck glanced up from the paperwork in his hands but said nothing. Not a wink of emotion showed on his lined face, a world-class poker player, if he were social enough to join a game. After all these years, I was certain Chuck never smiled once, never showed emotion at all.

He had to be married.

My old business pal gestured for me to take a seat, so I unfastened the lowest button on my suit coat to get comfortable for the steady stream of signatures. A piece of paper jutted out from the nearest folder, only inches from my fingers. I tapped it, but it didn't move. I pressed my lips thin and lifted the lid of the folder, tapping relentlessly on the edges of paper until the wayward sheet aligned itself.

Chuck glanced up and rolled his eyes. "Nick," he said, setting down the stapled packet. "I took a gamble on you all those years ago. My boss wasn't thrilled, but I convinced him. For you, I convinced him. Many changes have happened in banking since then. You've changed. I've changed. You look good, by the way."

"You do, too," I said, keeping a friendly spirit.

Chuck circled a pen above his head as if making an invisible sundae. "What's going on with the mop on your head? Get your ears lowered, kid."

I finger combed my longer locks and winked. "I'll keep it while I got it."

The loan officer glared for a moment but declined to comment on his wisps. "I'm not sure I like what I see here."

I pointed to the numbers on his copy of the last page. "The amount needed for several technicians and production staff is substantial, but NBB has plenty of assets for collateral. The projected revenues guarantee the loan can be repaid under standard repayment terms. I've analyzed the finances at various interest rates to show the bank's potential earnings. As you can see, issuing this loan is a wise financial choice for Stars National Bank."

"With your debt-to-income ratio, how do you think you'd qualify for another loan of this size?"

I slipped another stack of papers out of my briefcase. "Right here."

While the complacent man skimmed the text, his bushy brows popped. My knee bounced. Next to money, time was in short supply. What was taking so long? Chuck glanced at me while flipping another page. "This is interesting. What I see here is high risk, but where do these projected revenues come from?"

I raked a hand through my well-groomed locks. I deliberately left out the details of the contract out of necessity. But I did use the projected revenues not only from the upcoming first shipment payment, but the sales figures Chris had assembled in his marketing campaign that I had yet to approve. "I have a guaranteed project in the pipeline."

"These are forecasted revenues?"

I truly hadn't expected this much questioning. "Chuck, NBB hasn't let you down yet. I promise you, this project will deliver what you see. The contract is signed, but I'm not at liberty to discuss the details at this time."

The loan officer set the papers on his desk and folded his hands together, the grim line of his mouth making my leg bounce faster. "I have faith in your ability to run a good business."

I slipped a pen out of my suit coat, ready to sign and initial many pages.

"And these secret revenues are promising."

I smiled and sat up straighter.

"But..."

The worst word to hear at this stage. My leg bounced enough to shake the desk. What could possibly be the hang-up?

Chuck pushed the glasses back up his nose. "The financial statements you present show a margin too narrow for Stars National Bank's risk tolerance. Coupled with high inventory and no proof of this projected income, I cannot approve this loan."

I exhaled a deep breath like I'd been punched in the gut. Giving him my friendliest, most reassuring smile, I said, "I understand your concerns, Chuck. NBB has been in business for many years, and like all operations, some fiscal periods are quieter than others. This year it's our turn to shine. All I need is a relatively small loan to complete my project. Our business obligations and my loans with Stars National Bank are all current, with no risk of default. If you say yes, there's only reward for you."

The somber man passed my papers back to me. "I know the pitch, Nick. I've been a loan officer longer than you've been an adult, and I've heard everything. What I see are facts, and I cannot, in good conscience, grant you this loan. It's not personal. I'm sorry."

Not to be deterred yet, I said, "How can I prove I'm still a sound investment?"

Chuck stood. "You can go now."

I'd already invested too much for any other path but forward. I stood, heart pounding in my chest and echoing in my ears. I hated to do this, but I had no other recourse. "You know what you're risking by denying this loan, right? You're correct in reminding me I have several loans with Stars National Bank. The balances add up to a hefty sum, probably the highest in your portfolio. I'd hate to see any unnecessary default, and I bet your boss would be quite disappointed."

Despite threatening to default on my payments, Chuck wasn't to be perturbed. "It's not personal, Nick. Just business."

Tension tugged throughout my body. I aimed a finger at the loan officer to make my point clearer. "You're making a mistake."

The tight-lipped old man cracked a smile. "Then prove it."

If that was Chuck's attempt at motivating me to be creative, it worked. "This isn't over yet. When you see me next, you'll be begging me to sign."

I collected my materials, almost as harshly as Chris had done when he'd been turned down, and I added a personal door slam on my way out. I'd show Chuck Leach that at a cough away from forty years old, I was just coming into my stride. No matter what it took, I was going to succeed.

Failure was not an option.

II

Large Potatoes

I DROVE WITH NO destination in mind. I needed time to think. The golden ticket to success teetered precariously in the palm of my hand. If I couldn't find the funds to hire workers for Dr. Gibson very soon, if we failed to meet the government's deadline for the first shipment, that ticket was going to be ripped away forever. Burned. Never to be recovered. My working relationship with the government would be tarnished, likely over forever. And the government was a lucrative customer.

When the government did whatever it was going to do with The Annihilator, I needed to be the hero of the world with my Heromycin—*perfectly on the nose, Gibson.* But right now, that dream looked...bleak. How could I put on a smiling face for the public, knowing I'd failed them all? How could I, knowing the CDC handed my deal to my rival, Ted Bastard—I mean, Ted Bastion? I couldn't let that smug weasel win.

I could hear the cackling laughter from Dennis already.

If I couldn't get those bodies in marshmallow suits, my threat of defaulting would be a reality. A decent credit score was the only thing keeping me moving forward. Without it, I might as well apply for a waged position and kiss a boss's ass. For a flash, I pictured myself as Chuck Leach's assistant—slash—coffee guy, and a miserable frown pulled my features. After many years of working for myself, I could never do that. So, I needed to think, to figure out my next move. Every hour rolling by brought me one hour closer to the CDC's first deadline. The pressing weight of time on my shoulders had never been more ominous.

My department managers had nothing to cut, already been given a shoestring budget, and Heather Brush ordered too much cellulose that couldn't be returned but could be used on time—Flick's assumption. Anycillin was threatened with backorder status because of staffing issues. Profits were lower than expected. The bank refused to issue me another loan. I couldn't fire any more workers to fill the void, because I needed them to keep Anycillin afloat.

Glancing at my watch, I was out of time to give Chris the answer I'd promised. I dialed my older brother's office line and pinched the phone between my shoulder and ear while making a left turn. I really needed Bluetooth in my car one of these days.

"What do you mean 'no'?" Chris Barnes asked, voice strained with a familiar mix of anger and disappointment. Anger was easy to diffuse, but disappointment was a different beast entirely, and after facing it my whole life, all I'd managed to accomplish on that end was getting disowned by my parents. In hindsight, that wasn't terrible.

I clarified, "NBB doesn't have the money to finance your ad campaign right now. Hold on to it for a later date."

"You have the money for a fancy fish tank and a personal caretaker for it, a private floor in a lucrative real estate district in a building you own, but you can't find funds for ads that will increase your company profits? This is unbelievable."

Repeating Chuck Leach's motto, I said, "It's not personal, Chris. Just business. Don't make it personal."

Pent-up energy festered again. I wanted to blow off steam at the gym, but this was an inappropriate time of the day, and I'd prefer to have Andras there...

My lips pulled into a smile. I had *one* trick up my sleeve Chuck Leach didn't know about. I wasn't sure how effective it would ultimately be, but I was out of options. I knew exactly where to go.

"It is personal when it's your decision to make," Chris said into my ear. "And when your decision affects others, then it matters to them as well."

"My company is not a democracy."

I pulled into the ground level parking garage and stopped in my personal parking space. A chilly gust of wind smacked me in the face, but I didn't care. I entered my high-rise through the rotating glass front doors, and I avoided other people busy in the lobby. The portly security guard with his hands in his pockets nodded with a pleasant smile as if I were a celebrity, and I had to admit, it felt great. Soon, everyone was going to know my name.

When I reached the elevators, I jabbed the call button harder than necessary—better than smashing my phone in frustration.

"And you're not Mother Teresa," Chris said with an edge. If that was supposed to hurt my feelings, it didn't.

The line went dead in my hand before I could agree. Twice in as many days—something weird was happening between us.

On Andras's floor, I wove my way to my friend's office. Andras was on the phone, and after catching a glimpse of me, he waved me inside and hung up. "Hi, boss. What brings you down to my level?" The Chief Information Officer linked his hands together on top of his desk.

Seeing how clean and orderly my friend kept his office, even in the middle of the workday, I relaxed a little. I needed my head clear to properly navigate the next few minutes. "In the gym, you mentioned a partnership—a trade for power."

Andras File beamed. "I certainly remember. You've reconsidered?"

"Tell me more about Corson's deal."

The bulky man shifted in his seat as if excited. "It's easier to show you. Got an hour?"

I had a personal hard line I wouldn't cross, because a credit score and kissing a boss's ass was nothing compared to prison time. So before we proceeded any further, I leaned in for a confidential question. "It has nothing to do with the mafia, correct?"

Andras chuckled, and I wasn't sure if that was worrisome or not. "I assure you, it doesn't."

Breathing a sigh of relief that this Hail Mary pass wasn't already in the crapper, I texted Chelsea to reschedule all my conflicts for the next two hours, just to be safe. She immediately confirmed.

"I'm available. Where are we going?"

Andras tapped a few keys on his keyboard, likely blocking out time in his schedule, and rose. "This way."

I followed my friend down the hall, keeping stride with the man's longer gait. At an ordinary door marked as a utility closet, Andras slid his badge against the plain wall. No sounds of locks shifting, or entrance being permitted, followed the strange gesture. Just silence, which I expected, since there was nothing in here but a closet—according to the blueprints I'd studied before choosing the location of my secret lab. Andras's behavior was concerning, since he was normally attentive and on the ball. I asked, "Are you feeling okay today?"

My friend winked and opened the utility closet door for me. "Right this way."

With a dismissive shrug, I entered the darkened room. When Andras crossed the threshold behind me, a soft blue light outlined the shape of an interior door, but there wasn't any knob or frame. "What is this?"

My friend reached out to the edge of the blue light and tapped. What should've been a wall, or perhaps a hidden door, split open down the middle. The blue phosphorescence encompassed the entire opening, and brighter flickers danced like the fish on my reef. There was nothing in this closet that shouldn't be, but my eyes told me a different story.

What kind of technology made this glowing blue light, because it certainly wasn't a web of LED lights? If this was on my energy bill, whoever was responsible was going to receive a big surprise from Jason Flick—an invoice.

"What you seek is inside." Andras smiled and stepped into the glowing doorway.

Determined to understand the deal and discover real estate that had been hidden during the inspection process, I frowned and centered myself against whatever blue goo or fatal dose of static electricity was about to ruin my perfectly good suit. And if that happened, Andras was going to receive his own big surprise from Jason Flick.

12

Hidden Property

WHEN I CROSSED THE threshold, it simply closed behind me, extinguishing the light. I tugged on my sleeves and checked my pants. My suit survived fully intact. I checked my hands, but no residue clung to my skin. Well, that was pleasantly anticlimactic.

But where I expected endless rows of sterile hallways identical to those snaking around the NBB building, I found something else entirely. My jaw fell open at the stretching hall of arching stones before me. Fiery sconces cast flickering orange light down a path of darkness. I swiped the stones with a finger, half skeptical of my own eyes and half wanting to discharge any residual static electricity.

When I retracted my finger with a smudge of moss or mold, my back stiffened, and I sucked in a breath. Mold remediation was not cheap. This would reduce my real estate value. Even worse? The filth before me was real. I slipped the handkerchief from my suit pocket and cleaned my finger. I'd have to burn the handkerchief later, and I liked this one. Shame.

I wished for a paper bag to breathe into, but judging by the looks of this place, I was out of luck. "What's going on here? What is this place?"

"Down this hall is a room. We can have a seat, and I'll explain everything."

"Can you first tell me why there's a moldy damp dungeon hiding in a broom closet in the middle of my skyscraper?"

"Follow me."

I gritted my teeth at the thought of adding more filth to my shoes. I exhaled a deep breath, and my limbs jerked to life. I followed my friend until a high-pitched squeak came from around the corner. I startled before realizing it was just moving metal, and not mice. That was not a scurrying, gnawing cretin of the night hunting me. Nope. Not in the middle of my building.

"Are you okay?" Andras asked, hiding a sheepish grin.

"This place needs a cleaning crew and bleach—so much bleach!" The hairs on my arms lifted as if wanting to jump out of my own skin. I suddenly identified with my arm hair. That was a new low. "I don't think I can do this."

"You're doing fine. Just a few more steps." Andras's thick arm wrapped across my shoulders, ushering me forward. Up ahead, a door swung open, and a man in a chef's uniform pushed an empty rolling cart down the hall away from us. The metallic sound I'd heard! But I didn't really relax.

He'd left the door open, shining a brilliant light across the damp stone floor, and as Andras and I strolled by, I peeked inside. Endless rows of cubicles with people on headsets chattering with the cleanliness and orderliness I required in my building. Although the interior was familiar, I didn't recognize it.

"What department is that?"

"Customer service."

As a business-to-business company, my version of customer service was troubleshooting issues between the vendors and either accounting or purchasing. I wasn't aware I had actual customer service inside my own building, and since I wasn't aware of it, that was getting cut. There were a lot of employees in there—plenty for me to sacrifice for Gibson's lab. I smiled, happy to get the hell out of this filthy dungeon. "I think I've seen enough."

A different man in a chef's uniform pushed another rolling cart, this one with a tiered cake, into the customer service department. He closed the door, smothering the hall in darkness once again.

Andras's meaty arm gripped my shoulders more firmly. "It's just up here."

After a couple of turns down indistinguishable halls, a loud explosion shook the walls, sending dust and pebbles sprinkling to the ground.

"What was that?"

"Routine maintenance. Don't worry. Right through here." Andras stopped and gestured for me to enter a room through a rounded-top entrance. This whole secret area reminded me of a medieval castle's dungeon. Where had this area been on the blueprints? And why hadn't it been remodeled in what appeared to be *centuries*? I overpaid for this building. When I got back to the office, I was going to have a very unfortunate conversation with my real estate agent. Someone was going to pay for this grievous error.

Inside the room sat a pair of primitive hewn chairs and a single massive unfinished desk—not even a lamp. Not willing to touch the wall again, I looked for a light switch, but there wasn't one. "What's going on here, File?"

The behemoth, who I wasn't sure I knew anymore, lowered himself behind the desk and gestured for me to get comfortable. In the dark, I leaned in close to the chair to inspect it, knowing finding any comfort in here would be impossible. Light brightened the room. I couldn't find the source, like there were no bulbs, but I was happy for the comfort of light. I inspected the chair for dust, mold, and stability before sitting. I exhaled, realizing I had just entered my own personal hell.

"Welcome to Hell." Andras File linked his hands together on his desk, and a soft smile lifted his lips.

Adrenaline coursed through my veins, and if I didn't get to the gym soon, I was going to explode. Too many questions vomited at once, each one projecting more frustration and anger than the previous. "Explain to me what this place is and why it's in my building, and I want the truth. How do you have access to this area, but I don't? I can't believe this! Who were those customer service people? I never authorized their work function. I definitely would remember that many useless positions at NBB." I spun at the mossy horror. "And why is this place so filthy?"

"Whoa, hold on there." Andras chuckled, angering me further. "I already told you. This is Hell. That department back there was customer service, and they're not employed by your company." I was supposed to buy that lie. "For the rest—the glowing doorway is a portal to Hell, which means we aren't in your building at all. Now that you know what we are and where we are, I understand being down here is harder for you than most. Can you handle it?"

I wasn't handling it at all. "Let's get this over with as soon as possible."

"I have been granted permission to give you the official offer from Corson, The King of Hell."

"The *King*...of Hell?" I didn't know whether to laugh at the absurdity or call for immediate medical intervention. I was hallucinating and deep into a psychotic episode. It was that tumor resurfacing, growing, spreading. I dug out a cell phone from my pocket and checked the screen. "If this is Hell, why am I getting service?"

"Fiber optic is more reliable for us, but we do have Wi-Fi in some areas. This is Hell, not Mars."

"Ah yes, a trip to Mars, but in the wrong direction." I shook my head. It clearly needed to be examined. I dialed.

"Who are you calling?" Andras asked.

"I have to schedule an MRI. Should've done it before, but I'm not waiting now."

Andras rose and slowly pushed my phone down. "The red eyes you saw on me weren't reflections. They were as real as I stand before you."

None of this made sense. Pinching the bridge of my nose, I asked, "Are you saying you're The King of Hell?"

The bulky man laughed. "I can see how you'd jump to that conclusion, but no. I'm merely his acting agent today. He's busy. Look at me."

Considering looking anywhere else freaked me out, I did. Within seconds, Andras's eyes glowed red once again, and in this dungeonlike hellhole, it was simply terrifying. I didn't scream—at least I didn't think so.

"Let's say I believe you, that I don't, in fact, have an aggressive tumor chewing away at my grey matter. You're telling me I'm standing in Hell? Like fire and brimstone hell? Like biblical...?" I trailed off. "Am I dead?" I didn't remember dying, but I could've been poisoned. I tried to remember what I last ate or drank...

Andras's lips lifted with amusement. "You're not dead at the moment."

That wasn't a reassuring answer. "So where's the fire, torture, and screams of the damned?"

"Fire we passed in the hallways—remember the sconces? Torture and its accompanying screams are in the north wing," Andras said with the tone of a tour guide.

"It's cold down here." I rubbed a chill from my arms. I thought Hell was supposed to be hot.

"Colder people take longer to die."

My mouth opened to comment, closed, and opened again. "People? As in, not souls?"

"Have you tried torturing a soul?"

Uh, well, no. "Can't say that I have."

Andras smiled. "This isn't the Hell in your stories. In fact, you can forget anything you might have read. Since I know you, Nick, I'll let you in on a big secret—it's all fiction, written by bronze age men with a serious lack of understanding of geography and natural science. Play a few tricks on them, and there you have it."

My mom shoved all that crap down my throat my whole life. Although I never believed, I wanted to gloat about being right. But...I was standing here, in Hell, a real hell, supposedly. Did I owe her an apology? I wasn't sure. "All of it is fake?"

"Well." Andras twirled a wrist in the air. "Hell is real, clearly. So is Heaven, but they aren't what you think."

The leaky, moldy stone walls were pretty close to what I'd pictured. "There's no such thing as sins threatening our grace with God? No pride that's going to send me to...?" I trailed off, realizing where I stood.

"Only man's construct."

I got up and paced the dank room. All those years of lies! Dennis proselytized me endlessly, using his Good Book as an excuse to belittle and demean my choices. He'd claimed my desire to do better and be better were signs of corruption and selfishness. As a teenager, I couldn't make the connection; I didn't understand. Now I believed I did. Dennis had been only trying to manipulate me.

But why?

Even with the truth, I would never be able to change Dennis's mind, not that the man deserved the truth. And even if I demanded answers, Dennis would only dig in his heels deeper. The man was a stubborn bastard. I smiled to myself. Guess dear old dad was only projecting when he'd relentlessly called me the same thing. I was feeling a little bit epic...or a lot a bit smug.

"I'm afraid to ask what the smile is for," Andras said.

"A few things suddenly made sense." The last hour had tested my sanity. But as the pieces of the puzzle clicked into place, I had to wonder about the behemoth man before me. I had a feeling he didn't juice at all. "Can I ask you something?"

"Go ahead, but I might not answer."

This was entirely crazy, but considering where I stood, I took a chance. "Are you a demon?"

The large mass of a man stilled as stone. I wasn't sure whether I should poke him with a stick or run for my life.

EVENTUALLY, ANDRAS MOVED, AS if he'd telepathically consulted someone for permission for something.

"You need to sit down."

I glanced at the chair. "No, thank you."

"Suit yourself. I'm going to show you something, and you need to remember it's still me, okay?" Andras asked carefully, standing and approaching me.

"Uh, sure." What could possibly require a disclaimer?

Andras shimmered, like his form lost focus, and I blinked, but the blurriness remained. I rubbed my eyes and blinked again. Still, it persisted. I pulled out my cell phone and tapped the numbers for an ambulance. I shouldn't have skipped scheduling that MRI. Why didn't I listen to my own gut feeling? The phone wasn't ringing. I checked the corner of the screen and found no service. "Andras, I'm not feeling well."

I fell into the primitive chair and rested a hand on my forehead. Was the room spinning, too?

"You're fine. It's not you, it's me."

I craned my neck to follow the familiar voice, but Andras File was gone. A massive shiny...uh...some*thing* stood near me.

"Don't be afraid. It's still me."

My mouth fell open. My friend had worse issues than I did—a strange form of vitiligo, maybe, but instead of patchy altered pigments, Andras was...fully, completely...*purple*. No suit. Naked and covered in shiny scales, like a little girl's toy lizard. That must've been hard to deal with in high school. I rose, and my friend now stood over seven feet tall. "Man, I'm so sorry. I had no idea. How did you hide it so well?"

"It's a special trick. Not all of us can do it, but everyone in the customer service department can. You remember those miles of cubicles? Most of them hope to be promoted to Field Agent, where they'd be interacting with humans directly, but the ability to glamour is required."

I understood very little of that, but I pulled out my cell phone again and dialed.

"What are you doing?" Andras asked.

"You need an ambulance more than me, either for your condition or your mental health."

"There's nothing wrong with me."

I asked slowly, "Maybe NBB can find a cure. How many others suffer with something so...debilitating? No offense."

"Thousands, if not millions," Andras said flatly. I should've been afraid, but somehow, I only saw dollar signs. "Put the phone away."

"But..." The red, glowing eyes returned, and that was my cue to obey the giant, shiny, purple lizard. A swish of something darting through the air caught my eye. A tail?

"As I said, there's nothing wrong with any of us. I'm a demon."

"I thought red was the standard color. You're purple."

"And you're neurotic. Neither of us can help what we are, and I don't judge you for it."

I exhaled. After all this time, my friend was secretly a purple-scaled, shiny, iridescent lizard-demon. Maybe there was no cure for being a demon, but could they use a little prescription-strength antibiotic for the scales? I cleared my throat, hoping my capitalistic mind didn't anger my friend. "Everyone in that customer service department looked human. Do they all look like you underneath? You know what I mean."

"All demons look different, just like all humans are unique."

Maybe different varieties of prescription-strength antibiotic then.

I wanted to pace the small room to gather my thoughts, but I remembered the damp and moldy floor. Instead, I stifled a groan and returned to my seat. A real demon. "I'm in Hell with a demon, and I'm not dead," I summarized.

All this time, I had no idea—right in front of my face. Had I met any others? No one stood out, but before now, I had no frame of reference. The most obvious guess had me asking, "Is Lauren Hamil a demon?" That would explain so much. Not many guys could say their ex was a demon and mean it literally. I pursed my lips. Yep, a great party line. *This one time, I dated a demon...*

"She's human."

Damn. I'd hoped for a logical explanation for why my girlfriend rejected my proposal. What other excuse could there be for rejecting a full carat, lab-created moissanite, which was *better* than a diamond? Plus, she actually *liked* my parents, and she hated my fish. She had to be a demon. Damn. Lauren had turned out to be what I didn't expect—and still didn't understand.

I stared at my friend with wariness. All those months in the gym with Andras, swapping stories and sweat. All this time I'd trusted my Chief Information Officer to align interests with NBB. But all this while, my trusted best friend was a *demon*. What did that say about my choice of company? "Are you my friend, or was all of this some sort of ruse?"

"Let us settle our business before deciding what comes after."

I raked a hand through my long locks and carefully freed a knot. The humidity in the chilly dungeon caused my hair to frizz, and my patience for this mental episode or reality check was dwindling. The likelihood of my accepting anything from this *demon* sat around zero, but—assuming I believed all this—if Andras was my only answer to all my problems, I'd promised myself I'd do it. Since I wouldn't work with the mafia, how did demons rate on my personal risk tolerance curve? I chuckled at the ridiculousness of all of this. "Then what's Corson's deal?"

Andras blurred again, and after a few blinks, he shrunk back down to his beefy, suit-straining size and human color. The tail disappeared, too, and he returned to his seat behind his desk. Andras's familiar look and comforting smile helped me relax a little. Like a really tiny little. "On behalf of The King of Hell, I'm officially offering you the previously discussed deal: special power in exchange for cooperation and a commitment to the cause."

"Can you clarify 'special power'?" I was being patronizing, but after everything piled on me today, I didn't care, and after Andras's little costume exchange, I wasn't interested in becoming a giant, purple-scaled, shiny, iridescent lizard-demon. And since I didn't have a contract to read, I wanted all the fine print read aloud to me.

"First, you shall have the ability to read people like no one else."

I frowned. I was already astute in reading people, otherwise I wouldn't have managed to start and grow a pharmaceutical company with no support from anyone. It wasn't my fault I couldn't pick out a demon in a crowd. "Anything else?"

Andras leaned back in his chair, and a playful smirk shifted his features. "You shall wield fire."

Neat, but not useful. "So I'll be the go-to guy for all the smokers on break? Be the center of attention at the bonfire? Help the fire department with controlled burns?"

The demon—using that word seemed so wrong—leaned forward. "That's your choice. The fire is more like a 'get a free gift with purchase' situation."

Not satisfied but still curious, I asked, "Not to be greedy, but this deal was supposed to solve all my problems, and I'm not seeing it yet."

"Teleportation is industry standard."

Hmmm. Useful. As if that existed.

"And other things could manifest for you, but we aren't sure what they might be."

I wasn't sold. "What is the partnership part of this deal? The one that leads to a 'fun and easy life'?"

"In exchange for the ability to read people like no one else, wield fire, and teleport, among other smaller benefits, we will need you to identify humans with a certain cast to their auras." Whoo, more gibberish. "If you see white, it means pure and black means evil, as you may guess. They aren't useful."

"Then what are you looking for?"

"All the shades of gray are players in the game. It's a critical job and let me express how stressful these last few months have been."

"Well, I don't understand any of that."

"I would hope not." Andras stood and sat on the corner of his desk, facing me.

Supposedly I'd get a few fun, but useless, abilities, in exchange for pointing out certain people. The fun part made sense. I mean, teleporting instead of traveling through rush hour traffic? Sign me up. But I didn't see where the easy life part came into play. Or how any of this helped me at all. "Then what's the catch?"

A bark of laughter pierced the cool air. "You still hesitate. Remember my tale of Gertie, who declined her offer?" I recalled the lame story, so I nodded. "Do you want to be like Gertie, or do you want to be Nick Barnes, the most powerful human on earth?"

An intriguing pitch for some, but I wasn't convinced. "Why did she turn it down, exactly?"

Andras scratched at the scruff on his jaw. "Honestly, she never said why."

"How does reading people and wielding fire help me?"

Andras rested his palms on his massive thighs. "What do you want?"

I lifted my brows. "Are you offering me a blank check on favors?"

"No. Specifically, what do you need assistance with?"

Oh. Worth a try, though. "I suppose my most pressing issue is convincing the bank to issue me a loan."

Andras chuckled. "Is that all? I guarantee you'll have no difficulty attaining that goal."

Well, if a demon guaranteed it...

Then Dr. Tyler Gibson would get his geeks, and my contract milestones would bring in hefty paychecks. Chris would get to play with his cameras to position NBB as the global distributor of Anycillin—paving the way for Heromycin's introduction at just the right time. And then maybe I would send my parents a passive-aggressive fruit basket. Eh, probably too much effort for a pair of people who raised me to settle for mediocrity and disowned me for rejecting their ideals. "Sign me up."

Andras clapped his hands together and beamed. "I knew you were a smart one, my friend. I'm going to call for reinforcements for the procedure. In the meantime, get comfortable. Oh, forget I told you Corson's name. He's just the king, Your Highness, or The King of Hell to you. This is great! He's going to be so pleased!" My friend—glad that was clarified—slipped out the door before I opened my mouth.

What procedure?

And where did his tail go?

13

Procedure Room

ALONE IN THE DUNGEON-LIKE medieval room, I braved the filthy floor to hunt down the source of the light. With no electricity, the curiosity was too much to bear. Behind the massive desk, I found a long strip of light, like an old fluorescent, but with no ballast or bulb. I reached out to touch it, and the heat stung my fingertips—like fire without flames. I returned to the hewn chair. Considering I'd just seen a giant, purple-scaled, shiny, iridescent lizard-demon, electric- and flame-free burning light shouldn't be shocking. But I had nothing else to ponder while I waited. What was taking so long?

I pulled my phone out of my suit coat pocket to check the time and catch up on some emails, but I had no signal. Suppose when the demons tortured people, no one browsed online. And why *people*? Andras didn't explain why people were down here at all, only that they were tortured, not souls. I was pretty convinced that Easy Street song would work well.

Not that I wanted to test it myself.

The door to the dungeon room burst open, and I stood, both to place my back safely near the wall—but not touching, and to get a clear view of the door in case I needed to escape. I wasn't sure what I was going to see next. In strolled a short, stocky human-looking man in a suit with one hand tucked into a pocket and the other free swinging with his steps. He had the thick patch of gray-peppered dark hair of a man in his late fifties. The guy reminded me of a mysterious uncle—a serious businessman always off in exotic locations, but he'd sneak a lollipop to the kiddos when the parents weren't looking.

I was going to like this guy, especially if he had lollipops.

Andras followed him inside. Making a leap, I expected this short man was called Your Highness. The material of his suit was strikingly fine, and the king's keen eyes assessed me up and down at the same time.

"This is him?" the king asked, skeptically. I wasn't sure if I should take offense to that.

"He looks the same as he did during the news interview on TV, sir," Andras said respectfully and leaned back out of the room as if expecting more...demons...to arrive.

"You must be The King of Hell," I said, holding out my hand. "I don't know what I was expecting, but you...aren't it."

With alarm on his face, Andras quickly approached me and said, "Nick, be careful of your word choice."

"What? I saw what you are," I said to Andras. "So I expected someone enorm..." My gaze moved back to the king, and I trailed off. The short man in charge smiled gently—the most surprising thing I'd seen in the last...oh, twelve minutes.

"Am I not impressing you, son?"

"It's not that. Pardon my curiosity. I'm new to this demon thing. Please continue."

Andras said with a warning tone, "Nick—"

"Now, Andras, do not fret. This young man has given his consent," the king said softly. "Oh, that rhymes."

I frowned. The undercurrent of rude authority was blanketed with condescending sweetness. My opinion of the short man dropped a couple notches, and he didn't seem to have lollipops.

Andras smiled. "Good one, sir."

The king continued, staring at me intently. "But that boldness is certainly familiar. I believe you have discovered the human we sought. Let us begin, shall we?" The king clapped his hands, which apparently meant something, and he stuffed one hand back into his pocket. The other swung wildly as he marched away.

That was fast and quite confusing.

"Come this way to the procedure room, Nick," Andras said and led me down the hall and around the corner to another rounded-top medieval door, but the inside of this room froze me at the threshold.

The bright light was the only thing pleasantly normal about this room. The rest—nope, not happening. Not the sulfur and sweaty sock stench, the blackened marks on the walls, or the dental-style chair bolted to the center of the floor. At the back of the room was a row of dented steel cabinets. If I thought the halls needed bleach, this room screamed penicillin and gas masks. In all honesty, I wasn't sure Anycillin was up to the task.

The King of Hell was inside, reading through paperwork, and next to him was a rolling cart lined with shiny surgical implements. That, uh, that was even worse. "What's all this for?" I squeaked out at Andras.

I suddenly realized I was way over my head down here. Up there, back home, I was on a clear path to earning the world's trust, but down here, I was the water boy, hoping to touch the ball someday. Such an odd feeling. And mostly terrifying.

The King of Hell lifted his gaze and smiled brightly, as if I were talking to him. "Not sure I understand it myself, but this is everything Wildabeast requested. You needn't do anything but relax. Before you realize, the procedure shall be complete."

"You're a demon," I said to the short, stocky man, articulating my disbelief. Was his real form the same as Andras's shiny purple lizard, or was he...something else?

"Of course I am." The king set down the paperwork to give me his full attention. Leaning against the dented counter, he folded his fingers together and crossed his ankles. The relaxed position did nothing to ease my anxiety. Nothing in this room could ever calm me without a sedative, and good luck sticking a needle into my skin. I'd half expect it to be rusty. I shivered at the cold seeping into my bones and the utter disgust with the conditions down here.

"It's okay," Andras whispered.

Nothing about this was okay in any way. Oh, that rhymed. The king would be entertained.

"I might not appear intimidating, Nick," the king said to recapture my focus. "But I want you to understand the considerable determination needed to rise through the demon ranks. Skills mastery in swords, firearms, pyromancy, and strategy must be proven for a chance to challenge the king for the throne. If successful, the new ruler becomes imbued with the power of kingship, and very little on this planet can stop their will. All my challengers for the last seven centuries are dead. Understand now, I am not just a demon, but yes, I am one."

"You slaughtered all your challengers?"

"At the polls, yes," the king said brightly. "Now, sit down and we can get started."

My lips parted. That was not the type of power I had in mind, but with those skills, I could do anything I wanted. Andras hadn't been kidding about the benefits. "You're *giving* me the kingship power?"

The king sighed. "What part of *considerable determination* did you miss? Your deal with Andras was to receive demon power, not kingship power."

That was still more than any human had, but no matter how tempting the power might be, I had my own line I wouldn't cross, a certain level of vanity I couldn't drop. "I'm not going to turn purple, am I?"

The king darted a sharp look at Andras before returning his attention to me. Despite the hardness on the king's face, his voice was gentle. "Every breed of demon has a different appearance. You are born human, so you have no need to be concerned about your skin color or height."

"Tail?"

The king shook his head.

That helped tremendously, but my feet remained fixed on the threshold. "This...Wildabeast, who needed all those tools, what is it going to do to me, exactly?"

At the name, the king smiled with a warmth of affection. "Don't call her an 'it' to her face, for one. Treat her with respect, or she'll turn you into a mouse for entertainment."

I gulped. Now that was a horrifying thought. Surrounded by demons in the belly of Hell, awaiting a female beast to perform an ancient ritual. Just another ordinary day. Shaking my head, my stiff legs carried me to the chair. I sat and crossed my ankles, stomach swirling with air bubbles and trying to pretend this was an ordinary dental visit.

"Where is Wilda?" the king asked, turning toward the door.

"I'll retrieve her at once." Andras ducked out of the room, leaving me alone with the king.

"So, Nick Barnes." The King of Hell smiled and leaned against the dented counter, facing me. His fingers danced along the shiny implements on the tray as if deciding which one to play with. "No doubt named after your father."

While I puzzled the significance of Dennis in all this, the king lifted a pair of tongs. Since I hadn't signed a contract, this craziness had to be one big mental breakdown. I climbed out of the chair. Experimenting on me was way beyond whatever imaginary new line I'd just created.

"Where are you going?" the king asked with a hint of personal rejection.

I wasn't a toy or a test subject. And this was all one big crazy bag of cats. "I need fresh air."

FACING THE DREARY HALL of nightmares was better than risking a pair of tongs being shoved somewhere they didn't belong. Footsteps echoed on the stones underfoot while I attempted to make turns opposite of those that brought me here. Passing flickering sconce after sconce, making my best guesses, a door similar to the customer service department appeared on my left. I opened it, hoping to re-center my mental map or ask for directions.

Inside, a man in a dirty and torn suit was chained to the wall, while another man—demon?—in a glittery outfit and unicorn-colored hair held a Popsicle and a long barbecue skewer. I wasn't sure which was the scarier sight. The victim screamed, and I shut the door with wide eyes and allowed my legs to carry me out of there. Was I really in Hell? *The* Hell?

Despite the cold air, my pounding heart warmed me. My leather shoes clattered against the stone. Where was that glowing blue door...which had no knob and required Andras's ID badge to activate? After thinking about it, my efforts appeared to be in vain, but I wasn't a man to give up easily. Rounding a corner, I bumped into a familiar face.

"What are you doing out here?" Andras rested heavy hands of concern on my shoulders.

"I don't think I can do this." I gestured around him. "This isn't real, is it? Am I... Am I losing my mind?"

My friend leaned down to meet my gaze. "You're not crazy. What you see is real, but it's not as bad as you think. Let's return to the procedure room, and afterward, you'll be escorted back to your building safe and sound. You have my word."

His reassurance and those heavy hands moved my feet. In fewer steps than I remembered, we were back in the dreaded procedure room.

"And the man returns!" The king set down his paperwork again, as if he'd continued reading through it, knowing I'd be back. "Have a seat. This won't take long."

I slipped into the dental chair and checked my watch. I'd only been down here half an hour. I could've sworn several hours had passed. Holding the watch to my ear, the second hand ticked evenly. Huh.

"I'm here." The feminine voice turned my head.

A striking woman strolled in, wearing skin-tight black exercise clothes and snow-white sneakers. She towered over the king, just as I had. The definition in her arms and legs impressed me, and I wanted to ask about her gym routine. The textured style of her platinum blonde pixie had me curious about her products, too. I could honestly say I'd never been so fascinated by a woman at first glance.

The woman carried a brown wicker picnic basket in the crook of her arm, and she set it on the cart, next to the torture—I mean, medical—tools. I swallowed a lump in my throat. I either manned up and completed this procedure or went home, non-existent tail between my legs...and the laughingstock of an attractive woman.

"Nice of you to show up, Wildabeast," the king said with genuine enthusiasm.

The woman, who appeared strong enough to bench me, furrowed her brow. "The name's Wilda Rivers. Call me that one more time, and you can cast this spell by yourself."

"Sorry, sweetheart. You know how these things slip free," the king said in a sweet voice. I suspected an intriguing history between these two.

"Nick, this is the witch who will perform the procedure. Do not fret, you are in excellent hands."

Wilda shot the king a look of annoyance and rifled in her basket, setting out herbs, glass beakers, liquids of various colors, and a leather-bound worn book. A real witch and an actual spell? Demons, now witchcraft. What the hell?

Andras simply stood guard at the door, as if expecting me to run off again.

"How was your trip from Chicago?" the king asked her.

She shook a vial of orange liquid and squinted at the meniscus. "Fast, when it works."

"I'm glad you had no difficulty getting here. Have you calculated your success rate with this spell?" And with that question, my concern returned.

"Eighty-two percent after three trials, but since I used non-human subjects, results may vary. You know my policy."

The king scribbled on his paperwork, and I suspected he was documenting the procedure, but that success rate had my insides turning to jelly. And we hadn't started yet.

I lifted a finger in the air. "Uh, I don't know the policy."

Ignoring my concern, the king said, "Better than your usual average. Wonderful! Nick, you're in wise hands."

They didn't feel wise.

Wilda laughed, offering hot pink sunglasses to the king. "Don't flatter me. It doesn't work."

"Yes, it does," the king retorted, accepting them, and placing them on his face.

Andras crossed the room and accepted his pair and put them on. The demons looked ridiculous wearing them, but a new concern struck me. "Do I get a pair?"

Once again, I was ignored.

Wilda said, "Are we ready to get this started?"

The king shook his pen. He scribbled viciously and grinned. "Yep, I'm good."

"Uh..." I muttered.

"Lie back and close your eyes," Wilda told me. "Everyone, make sure your seat backs and tray tables are in their full upright positions and fasten your seat belts. Here we go! Oh, I almost forgot again. Cell phones, please." Wilda held out her hand expectantly. The king and Andras turned theirs over, but I didn't move. Wilda flicked her fingers to urge me to give it up.

"Why?"

"If you want it to survive the next few minutes, hand it over. Magic has a way with electronics." I stared, unable to make heads or tails of that. She added in a childish voice, "Makes them go boom. If you no like-y, give me."

With a frown, I handed mine over. She placed them all in her basket and closed the lid. "Lead-lined. They're safe in there. Mine's in there, too."

"What's going to happen?" I asked, anxiety level like a rubber band stretched too thin and about to snap.

"Hopefully, nothing." She turned pages in her book. "That's what the basket's for."

"No, I mean, what are the steps of the procedure? Usually medical practitioners walk the patient through all the steps to calm the patient."

"Corson, didn't you fill him in? I don't have time for this. Just relax, tough guy. I'll be reading some words, rubbing a paste of animal innards on you, flicking some fluids at your face... Nothing too major."

"Sweetheart, don't call me Corson," The King of Hell said, and Wilda winked at him.

"Now sit back and relax," the witch told me. "The more you fight it, the more it'll hurt. At least, I think so, because of the squealing and claw thrashing during my testing phase."

I jackknifed upright and swung my legs over the torture chair. "I can't do this."

"Sure you can, tough guy. Stay calm or the king will have restraints brought in." Wilda's hand pressed me back down with little effort. I would've been impressed if I weren't terrified. I struggled harder.

"Wilda, that won't keep the boy calm," the king warned. "Nick, this is a standard operating procedure. Wilda is a professional. Don't be alarmed."

Wilda laughed. "You're funny, old man."

I craned my neck at the blond. "Which part was funny?"

Wilda shot me an impatient glance, and before I protested further, a mix of foreign words floated like a melody through the air, relaxing my every muscle. This wasn't so bad after all. She was right. I could do this. I lifted my legs back into position and leaned back, relaxed.

Then the pain started. Searing, blinding pain seized every moving structure in my body, all the way down to my toe hairs. Everything stood on end. My jaw gritted, and I tried to decipher the words, but my ears rang as if I were in an echo chamber with air horns.

The chanting paused, giving me a short-lived relief, and I panted.

"Did you bring the mouth guard?" Andras asked.

"I didn't have time to pop to the shop beforehand," Wilda said. "He'll be fine. If he needs new teeth, that's not my problem. Nothing was mentioned about the preservation of various body parts or functions."

The king growled. "He needs to live and be functional, or this is all pointless."

"People can eat without teeth. I've seen it," she countered.

I didn't like the sound of that, but since my body was still rigid as a board, I couldn't protest.

"Hang in there, my friend," Andras said with a pat on my shoulder. "You can do this."

I remembered nothing else but the burning pain roaring through my body as if I'd fallen into that flameless fire and swallowed a dozen rusty knives. The visual sent my heart pounding so loud it drowned out the chanting of the foreign words. I didn't know what would kill me first: a heart attack from the anxiety or a heart attack from the pain. I wished I'd learned why Gertie turned down this offer, but now it was too late to ask.

14

The "Gift"

MY VISION RIPPLED LIKE I was underwater behind a wall of lumpy glass. The rough stone of the walls reminded me of my reef rockwork. I smiled and visualized my fish coming to greet me, curious like puppies, but instead of asking for food, the fish wanted me to join them in play. Together we swam through and around the arches, and water flowed along my body like a silk sheet. The tentacles of an anemone teased my skin, and I didn't feel its stings when I slid a hand against the gentle flesh.

The fish warned me to avoid the wave makers near the end of the tank. I didn't know why. The current was a fun challenge. The fish sped up and zipped around a toadstool and headed back the other direction. Left behind, I shifted around, searching for the danger as I drifted closer to the end of the tank. The thrumming of the wave maker up ahead had me frantically paddling in the opposite direction, but I couldn't fight the current. My shoes were waterlogged. My suit was tugging at me. The current pulled me toward the fan blades and dragged me along the jagged rocks as if I were keelhauled. Every nerve in my body screamed.

I sucked in a breath, but water didn't fill my lungs—instead a bed of needles dragged fire in and out with each breath. I blinked and reality cleared around me—or more accurately, what I'd hoped was a bad dream. The King of Hell, Wildabeast, Andras, and the dental torture chamber came into focus. Hell, I'd take that brain tumor right about now. Oh wait, I *was* in Hell, literally, but also figuratively. I lifted a pulsing, hot hand and watched my finger twitch. Each spasm brought a reddish glow from within. Only Wilda, leaning over my face, tore my attention away from the horror before me.

"What—what is this? What did you do to me?" My shallow breaths burned. My body ached like I had actually been thrown against jagged rocks, and the heat glowing within—the only thing painless—scared the living piss out of me.

The intimidating blond leaned back and slapped my cheek, but something sharp sliced across my flesh like a pair of razor blades. "Ow! Damn," I yelled.

While I waited for the tear-inducing pain to recede, Wilda straightened and smirked.

"Why did you slap me? Did I...touch you or something? I don't remember doing it, but if I did, I'm sorry." Very sorry. That woman had a slap like an Olympic discus thrower.

"No, honey. You're fine. You're more than fine. Congratulations, Nick. You survived," the witch said and leaned over me again. She searched my face and poked at me as if inspecting a lab rat for results. She wiped my injured cheek while I swatted her away. "Hold still. I missed a spot."

"What happened?" I asked, remembering nothing but the initial chanting.

Off to the side, Andras stood defensively—as if I was about to take a practiced swing at him. Only this time, he gripped a large butcher knife, and my eyes widened.

"The procedure was...a success." Wilda exchanged glances with the king and Andras.

"Why the hesitation?" I searched myself for puncture wounds but found none, and Andras set the knife on the tray with a soft clatter. The giant, purple-scaled, shiny, iridescent lizard-demon, in a human shape with a suit, smiled at me, a true and kind smile, but his eyes shined a brilliant red again.

"Why, uh, why are your eyes glowing, Andras?"

"Oh, honey. Whenever a demon is emotional, the red glowies come out." Both Andras and the king protested her description, but Wilda laughed. "Touchy males. But you, my dear, are something special."

"Wilda, we discussed this," the king warned.

"Discussed what?" I asked. The way Wilda said 'special' reminded me of days I wished I could forget. In middle school, but more prominently in high school, the principal dragged me and Chris into his office, both of us sporting some fresh bruises. Chris and his friends had teased me for selling comic books and Pokémon cards out of my car instead of joining the football team—apparently the only way to show I was 'cool', just for the record. Every time Mom heard the story from all three sides, she would always say I was special. It never came across as a compliment, though, but I never thought much else of it. The coincidence was probably nothing.

Ignoring my question, Andras said, "The important thing is you made it through, Nick, despite the odds of one in several million."

"One in sixty-seven million, to be precise." Wilda carefully inspected each of her spellcasting supplies and slowly packed them into her wicker basket. "Let's not underestimate the level of special here."

There was that 'special' word again. More important than a word from my childhood stinging was the knife Andras had wielded while I was unconscious. "What was the knife for?"

"Insurance," Andras said.

"Well, what matters is the boy wonder lives," the king announced, setting down the papers and his pen. "Excellent work, Wilda. I owe you a favor, lest we forget."

"I won't forget something so valuable. Good luck, Nick. I'm out of here." With that parting statement, the witch collected her picnic basket and tossed my cell phone onto my lap, sending a spark of pain through tender nerves. After tossing phones to Andras and the king, Wilda sashayed out the door. I watched her firm backside shift under the tight nylon, and my hand caught on fire.

I yelped, but quickly realized it didn't hurt. I flipped my hand back and forth, watching the flames lick my skin without marring me. I didn't even feel the heat. "I'm…I'm… What is this? What's going on?" I checked my clothing, and the sleeves and edges of my once fine suit were charred. "What happened to my suit?"

The king chuckled, amused. "Fear not, this is all normal, but we'll get you trained."

Andras whispered, "Sir, what part of this is normal?"

The king hushed him and left.

While the flames continued to flicker on my skin and singe my sleeve, I forced in a breath and asked my friend, "None of this is normal! What happened to me?"

Andras leveled a palm on my shoulder. "You're the first human to be turned into a demon...successfully...with hiccups. Frankly, we did not expect success."

I glanced at the fat blade resting on the table. "You were going to kill me if it didn't work?" The flames climbed up my arm and my wool suit shrunk and curled away, stinking of burned hair. Andras's hand and suit were unaffected, but how? The phone in my sore lap reflected the flames. I tossed it onto the counter to preserve it.

Andras solemnly nodded. "When a spell fails, sometimes the results can be perilous, and the only way to preserve the subject's integrity is to absolve them of their current corporeal status. Sometimes we allow the failure to complete to feed the hellhounds. It's just a matter of demand for the food versus the hours of housekeeping required to prepare the room for the next subject."

"Integrity? Corporeal? Are you saying the spell could've blown me to pieces?"

"In a manner of speaking, that outcome was unlikely."

I couldn't believe my own ears. "Like struck-by-lightning or bitten-by-a-shark-in-Kansas unlikely?"

Andras tilted his head in silent calculation. "More like...will-it-be-windy-today unlikely."

"I don't like those odds."

Andras smiled. "But you beat them, so again, congratulations!"

"You said I was successfully turned into a demon. Did you mean I was gifted demonic power—the read people, wield fire, and teleport deal? That's what you really meant, right?"

Andras pressed his lips together. "I'm afraid not. You're a bona fide demon with all the abilities that entails. But don't worry, we'll get you trained, as we said, and this flaming issue"—Andras gestured at my hand, still ablaze—"will be controlled. You'll be able to blend in with humans easily."

With one simple but painful curse, I was a demon, which I didn't know was possible. Hell, I didn't know demons truly existed until Andras showed me. Now I was one of them. Anger flowed through me like molten lava. The flames increased exponentially, and Andras backed up—in the direction of the knife, I noticed.

"You said this deal was a special power in exchange for following undisclosed rules and a commitment to Corson. Turning me into a demon was never mentioned, and I didn't sign any agreement. If there was fine print—trust me, with a handful of attorneys in my pocket, I know enough to read the details—but you deliberately kept that information from me. How could you do such a thing without my approval? This is an outrage!" Flames consumed me, adding shades of orange tones to my vision.

Andras stopped, back pressed against the dented steel cabinets. "Would you like a refund?"

"This isn't a joke. You deliberately manipulated me into becoming this...this...this thing." Flames grew beyond my body and swallowed the chair. My suit pressed against my skin, shrinking in the heat. "What have you done?"

"These are dire times, Nick. We must do whatever is necessary for the right reasons." Andras made a placating gesture. "Now I'm going to need you to calm down."

"I'm a sacrifice? For what?" I stood. My breaths became shallow pants against the clothing constricting my chest. Efforts to drag in air were futile, but at least the needle-scraping pain eased.

"More like a scout."

"What the hell...is going on...here?" I grasped at my tie, furiously loosening the melting polyester, and I tore open my pressed button-up shirt. Buttons popped, and I spread the fabric, but still, I couldn't breathe.

"You need to calm down, Nick."

"Don't tell me what to—" I cut off my own words. Roaring fire consumed my vision. I couldn't see. I couldn't breathe. My expensive suit was destroyed, and I had been manipulated like a child. Like Chris taunting me into fights and accusing me of starting them. Like Dennis blindly taking golden child Chris's story for face value. My pleas for understanding and sympathy were lost in the breeze. I had no control.

Andras covered his ears.

A thunderous boom shook the walls, and a fireball exploded in every direction. Andras's hair blew back, and his suit jacket and pant legs fluttered with the force, but he was otherwise unaffected. Everything around the room was blackened, and tendrils of steam floated up from all the surfaces. Dust and pebbles sprinkled down from the stone ceiling. I crumpled to the icy floor, finally able to breathe, and I dragged in deep, relieving breaths. My watch was still on my wrist, but I was too exhausted to inspect its condition. My clothes were shredded, melted, a burned mess on the stone.

I was naked.

Never had I been so humiliated. Not when Dennis ranted at me for a mistake in front of all Chris's friends. Not when the girl I'd taken to the Spring Fling ditched me for the lacrosse goalkeeper. Not even when my adult friends told me they were thrilled for my second entrepreneurial venture, bound to fail, and laughed behind my back. Oh yeah, I heard it and still had to face them every day. None of those times measured up to my emotions exploding out of control, leaving me like this in a Hell dungeon, cold and naked.

"Well then, your trainer has her work cut out for her," Andras said lightly. "I'll fetch you a proper suit. Try to stay calm. Otherwise, the flames will return."

"Trainer?" The king had mentioned that. From the owner of a leading pharmaceutical company respected by the government and looked up to by thousands, now I needed help to control my own emotional outbursts like a damned toddler.

I followed the grooves in the stone with my finger. Char clung to my fingertip, and I rubbed at it, but it still lingered. Anything alive in this room—whether moss, mold, or insects—was now dead, incinerated. Except for the demon standing beside me, immune to that which destroys. "Are you...am I...dead?"

"You're not dead at the moment." Andras repeated gently.

Great, so there would be more opportunities.

Andras paused in the doorway. "As a walking torch and an explosive with a short fuse, we cannot have you roaming the streets. Humans fail to understand these things, and we don't need mass panic."

The ridiculousness of the whole situation brought out my snark. "Right, sure. Whatever you say. If my watch melts, you're replacing it."

Andras approached and placed a hand on my bare shoulder. "The more your emotions control you, the more the fire grows. Without control, it acts as a defensive shield, which can get out of hand, as you see."

I was afraid to ask, but having information was better than finding out the hard way. "Defense against what?"

"Sit tight while I get your clothes and trainer." Andras File left.

I remembered the blackened marks on the walls when I'd entered this torture room. Now there were significantly more, and they were extra dark, refreshed. What happened down here before me? More humans getting turned? More spells? More explosions?

I must've been special. Unlike the others before me, my explosion destroyed that god forsaken dental chair.

My friend, a demon, had brought me to Hell, and a witch turned me into a demon. The only benefit I noticed was fire killed germs. Not very useful in my day-to-day life unless I needed to save on soap or wanted to replace my furniture every day. Andras's words popped into my head, *We will need you to identify people with a certain cast to their auras.* What did the shades of gray even mean? *It's an essential job.* If you say so.

If any of these demons expected me to walk away from my company for any kind of 'essential job', they were out of their minds.

A rap on the doorframe turned my head. The person walking in, whose high heels made an obnoxious clatter against the stone floor, was the last I'd expected. And I seriously thought I couldn't be more embarrassed.

15

She's Back

A SMUG HEATHER BRUSH with her black locks secured in a serious bun, wore her usual sleek pencil skirt and a well-tailored suit coat. The red lips were still in place as if she'd just walked out of a meeting at NBB. Somehow, I had a feeling I'd regret having fired her.

"I would've welcomed you earlier, but it sounds like we've been a bit of a pill for you to swallow," Heather said with a bold smirk on her face.

"You could say that again. Is Andras coming back? He was bringing me clothes."

Heather made a point of staring at me, folded on the dank floor, cupping myself for a scrap of dignity. I couldn't tell if the smirk was her personality or her reaction to me. Flames enveloped my hands once again, and I yelped in panic, exposing myself to her fully. After a moment's thought, the flames hadn't hurt my junk, and I exhaled deeply a few times before slowly moving my trembling and burning hands back. This seriously couldn't get any worse.

"Not such a toughie down here, are you?" Heather chuckled at my expense. Just great.

"Safe to assume you're a demon?" That explained a lot, honestly. I awkwardly rose to my feet. Despite the circumstances, I felt like I could handle this better when I towered over her. Flames grew from my hands, sweeping up my arms, and I didn't—couldn't—fight it.

Heather laughed. "All this time I put up with an arrogant ass. Now I get to watch a flaming one squirm."

"I'm glad you're enjoying this," I said, dryly. If I wasn't already on fire, I was sure I'd be blushing.

Heather strolled around me as she said, "As you said before axing me in front of my friend, can you think of any *ass*-ets that can be spared?" She paused, pointedly assessing my naked ass. Flames traveled farther along my skin. "There is a particular ass running through my mind right now."

"Very funny. Look, I did what I had to do. If you wanted to do your job, I wouldn't have fired you."

"Well, I'm doing my job now. I see plenty of 'raw materials'." She circled around to my front and stared at my body. "But there's definitely a 'shortage' in sight." She laughed, and flames engulfed my face. "I'm guessing in your current state, you won't need...'expedited processing'." She emphasized the last two words.

I caught the double meaning and checked myself. I was firmly covered. "Is this necessary?"

"Oh, for me it is. Perhaps if you didn't fire me in such a humiliating way, I wouldn't be doing this. Next time, I don't know, consider how others feel when you rip them from their livelihoods and toss them on the street."

"That's not fair," I said, really wishing for a fresh suit right about now. "Why did you order so much cellulose without knowing for certain it would be backordered?"

"Is that what this is about? You're upset about me stocking up? Didn't Production have trouble getting orders out the door on time?"

"They did," I said slowly.

"I stocked up."

I exhaled, and surprisingly, my lungs were immune. "I don't know what to say."

"It's okay to be wrong. It's better to admit it. But you were right about one thing. I much preferred getting laid off than to work for you any longer. The king wasn't thrilled about me losing my assignment, but he got over it."

A slice of guilt and a squirt of insult completed the shit sandwich. "I could've been nicer about it. I could've given you more time to explain and help me out of a sticky spot, but in my defense, I offered to do it privately."

Heather made a playful but dismissive noise. She wasn't satisfied.

"I'll admit I'm out of my league here. You know more than me. You're stronger than me." I assumed. "I'm sorry. Can you *please* bring me some clothes?"

Heather made another circle like a restrained predator. "I love it when you beg."

Andras returned with a suit folded and stacked and a pair of shiny shoes on top. I couldn't have been happier to see him, until he handed the stack to Heather. I stifled a groan, hoping she wouldn't destroy them out of spite.

"Good luck, my friend. See you on the other side." Andras left again before I could protest.

Heather tossed the stack onto the charred and melted dental chair. "Get dressed. We have work to do."

"I'm still burning. How do I stop it?"

"It's fireproof. Now get dressed."

Huh. I grabbed the stack, and the fabric danced slightly in the waves of rolling heat but didn't ignite. Cautiously, I held it against my junk for privacy, waiting for Heather to turn around.

Heather rolled her eyes. "I've seen everything there is possible on a human man."

"Cool. I'm not them."

She rolled her eyes and turned her back to me. "I didn't take you for a modest man."

"I'm not when I'm around people, but you don't qualify as people."

"Neither do you, dear."

I ignored that and dressed quickly before Heather's patience waned. Impressed with the material, I laced the shoes and snugged the tie against my throat. I shook my shoulders to loosen the layers. The vicuña had my lips spreading in a smug smile, and I caressed the powerful, luxury fabric. I tugged the sleeve over my watch, and I finally noticed it had melted. I sighed, but at least I felt like myself again for the most part. In fact, something about this suit brought out a strength I'd forgotten since walking through that glowing blue portal.

"Is this suit cursed, too?"

"That is the most idiotic thing I've heard today."

"I'll take that as a no."

"Why? Feeling...different?"

Annoyed she could read me so well, I grumbled, "Now what?"

"Nicky, Nicky," Heather said with playful amusement.

Flames expanded from my arms and torso to my face, turning my sharp vision orange. "Don't call me Nicky."

"I think I'm going to, Nicky, but I'm sensing a story there."

Heather pushed my buttons on purpose, but even still, the insubordination angered me, and flames rolled down my legs, engulfing my entire body. My mom called me Nicky. Every time I went to her for help, for defense, for reassurance, she'd always redirected me to Dennis. I'd never gotten that respect from her. I never had that trust she'd stand up for me. I was on my own for as long as I could remember. And every time that name was thrown my way, it was a constant reminder of how dead I was inside.

"It's none of your business." On an ordinary day, I'd never take physical action against a woman, even if completely deserved. As if the intimidating blond witch had unlocked the cage on a questionable inner subconsciousness, that scruple no longer burdened me. I smirked.

"I am loving this," Heather said. "Now, in the middle of my taunts, I need you to calm yourself instantly. The flames will vanish when you succeed."

"Why should I? The urge to smack your smart mouth is so strong, so very strong."

Heather shook her head. "That's the demon talking. Unlike you, I was born a demon. I've had time to discover myself and choose where I fit in over decades and centuries. But you don't have that luxury, so we need to fast forward your demon puberty."

"Please don't call it that." The flames grew.

"Millennia ago, demons had little regard for humans, like you're showing now, and that caused a catastrophic event among the humans. We had to eliminate them with fire and brimstone."

Remembering Dennis's endless speeches about obeying God and the subsequent destruction of two entire cities, I made the leap. "Are you talking about Sodom and Gomorrah?"

"You've heard the tale?" Heather raised her brows.

"Unfortunately."

"The result was so horrifying, demons and angels were united as one in a vow of secrecy. So understand, that vow not even you will be permitted to break."

"Angels are real?" My face slackened with disbelief.

"Is it so hard to believe? You're talking to a demon. You've been converted to one. Nature needs balance."

If angels and demons were real, then all I could hope for was Dennis's just punishment someday. "Is God real?"

Heather smirked. "If you want to fix your company's problems—which I'm guessing weren't solved by firing me—you need to control yourself. Or you can kiss that life you've built goodbye. Time doesn't run the same down here as it does up there. Tick tock, tick tock, Nicky."

THE FRUSTRATING DEMON WAS right—I couldn't waste time asking questions. I had to figure out this flame situation so I could get topside. I needed to find the cash for Dr. Gibson's geeks, so I could make that first shipment. I didn't have time to figure out my chaotic fire. I just had to do it. Besides, my fish needed to be fed. They were probably worried about me—more likely, why they hadn't had dinner yet. My flames vanished.

"Good. That's a start. Controlling your emotions means choosing which voice in your head to listen to. Take a moment to process and make sure you choose wisely." She'd make a decent therapist. "Now for a test. Nicky, when Lauren dumped you, did your family berate you for another in a long string of failures? I bet that was a fun argument—I mean, conversation."

I understood the game, but images and screaming words rushed into my head like a TV on full volume. I gritted my teeth, and flames ignited over my fists. I didn't want these voices. They needed an outlet. A place to go. Anywhere but in my head.

"Did your family plead with you to quit your evil job, get married, and have all the babies?" Heather pushed out her lower lip, mocking me. "They want you to be the good daddy, taking care of his family, dealing with a stressful boss, but you can't quit! Oh, no, the baby needs her checkups, and you can't go without insurance. But that's what makes a real man. Working hard, getting dirty, and bringing home that hard-earned, measly paycheck just to spend it on formula and diapers."

As if a match was flung into a puddle of lighter fluid, flames engulfed my body in a whoosh.

"Keep calm," Heather instructed. "Let the words bounce off you. Pay attention to your body and how you feel. Only you can choose how you react to those words. If you shield yourself against them, they have no power."

Dennis's wretched voice echoed between my ears. *It means you're a failure, you ungrateful, stubborn bastard.* The flames licked higher up my arms. My muscles tensed, wanting to release this strain, wanting to throw it at his face. Why did he hate me so much? Anger rolled through my veins, heating my core with that familiar tension on the verge of explosion.

I couldn't explode. I had to get home. *Let the words bounce off you,* I reminded myself, so I searched for something to grasp onto, something calming—Lauren, no. My parents? God, no. (Heather hadn't answered me if there was one yet). Chris—no way. Andras's glowing red eyes, uh—no.

I'm sure mine glowed, too.

The only thing I had in my life that was soothing was my reef. The cavorting fish weaving through the arches of rock. The fingers of coral dancing in the waves. The gentle hum of the equipment. I even pictured myself swimming with them again but deliberately left off the end of my daydream or hallucination—whatever it was. With a content sigh, the flames dissipated.

"Excellent." Heather clapped her hands like a mini cheerleader and approached my rigid body, heels echoing against the stones. Her hand slipped in the gap between the buttons of my shirt and caressed my chest, twirling and tangling in my hair.

I cringed. "Can you stop touching me?"

Heather grinned. "It's all part of your training."

"I know I can be irresistible, but what purpose does groping me serve?"

"Ha! God, that ego of yours is disgusting. So let's fix that a little, shall we? That secret government contract you're so desperate to fulfill? Oh yes, I know all about it, Nicky, and it will fail. Dennis is right. Dennis is always right." Flames returned, and for once, I wished they burned Heather's probing hand. "Milestone after milestone will come and go. Chris's silly attempt to rejuvenate sales will go nowhere but on your credit card. Eventually, you'll be so far beyond bankrupt, you'll be forced to foreclose on the NBB building and leave behind your poor fishes. You'll never see another bureaucrat's desk so long as I live, you egotistical, germophobic, OCD freak—"

My anger exploded in every direction, cutting off her insult train. The force rattled the stone walls. Dust fell from the ceiling, and I shook my hair. Heather's clothing and hair blew as if I were a bomb, but like Andras, she remained standing.

"Keep your hands off me," I warned. "And how do you know about my contract?"

She tsk-tsked me like a child, while she tugged her suit coat straight and smoothed flyaway hair from her bun.

"Have you forgotten what I just taught you? People are going to push you. Others will threaten you. For the secrecy of our society, you need to maintain control in the presence of the human population. It's essential. Now, let's try some offense." Heather returned to groping, hands sliding up my chest and tugging beneath my belt. Flames returned.

The only offense I wanted was to shove her clear away. "The deal was this power in exchange for identifying humans with shades-of-gray auras, whatever that means.

And as long as I'm following Corson's rules, whatever they are, I have no need for offense." Although the idea of tossing a fireball at Dennis had its merits.

"You know the biggest rule. For millennia now, we must continue to keep the hidden world hidden. Other factions have tried otherwise and failed. As have we. Unlike humans, we remember our history, and we *don't* repeat it. As far as offense goes, do you show up to the congressman's office without a pen? Do you walk into your managers' meeting without an agenda? I need you to focus your anger, panic, anxiety, and fears—everything that threatens your functioning like a well-oiled machine."

"I'm always prepared. It's the anxiety in me," I said dryly.

"I know it's hard to focus all those obnoxious emotions, especially for you, but channel them all into your hands and throw them at me."

"How do I...?" I trailed off, staring at my open palms, flame free.

"Focus. You must figure it out."

I remembered all the inflammatory words she'd thrown at me, the stinging insults from my parents, the cold callous remarks from my brother, the years of coffee pot chatter snaking around the office about how the whole company feared and hated me.

Despite Chris balking, I really needed to assign a mental health webinar for my employees. The frustration they held for me was unjust. They didn't understand the pressure I was under to make everything work—to make sure they had jobs to return to each day. They had no idea I could help save the world. Those ungrateful...bastards...

Roiling anger filled my body. I stared at my hands, willing it all to accumulate into my palms, and the pain, the struggle, the fight, coursed through my veins, as if following my orders. Fire sparked to life in my palms, and I focused, willing it to become something tangible, and it quickly increased in size and matter. Soon the flames materialized into a sphere, and I grasped it like I would a flaming basketball.

Remembering Heather's creepy, unwanted hands on my skin, I launched the fireball at her chest. Upon impact, it exploded into a wall of flames, throwing Heather backward into and through the stone wall. Dust billowed around the claustrophobic room, and a mossy scent rushed in from the next room.

Did I just do that?

My fire vanished with no remaining fuel to maintain it. Using my sleeve—in perfect, burn-free condition—I blocked the dust from my nose and mouth. Loose stones tumbled, and a rain of pebbles pattered the floor and tinkled on the metal cart. The dental chair of torture survived the blast, but I wasn't certain if my target did.

"Heather?" I stepped into the hazy hole and waved dust from my face.

A woman's cough came from the next room, and my teacher took wobbly steps with her high heels over the pile of loose debris. I held out my hand to assist her, and she accepted.

Heather emerged with a grin. "Excellent work. You need much more practice in defensive control, but your offense is most agreeable. Who knew all those broken gears up there were functional, after all?"

A pat on the back, followed by an insult. One of those was easy to brush off, and the other I'd heard over and over, easy to ignore right now. "I have a company to run. Am I done now?"

"We need you, Nick Barnes. The world is in a constant push and pull between the demons and the angels, and when we need your assistance, we will come for you. Opting out is not an option."

"The shades of gray thing?" I surmised.

"It's important. Follow me, and I'll lead you to the topside portal."

I kept stride with the woman down the hallway, which no longer felt cold, just damp. Even the darkness wasn't so dark any longer. As if someone reduced the contrast, I saw nooks, crannies, and cracks. I sucked in a breath while searching the corners of the stone floor as our feet ate up the distance. Why didn't my fear of mice leave with a chunk of my inhibition? "So we're all demons," I said to myself, reality sinking in.

"Some quick things you need to know—only demons can voluntarily come and go from Hell. Anyone else will trigger alarms, so don't invite a bunch of friends to party down here. We're all fireproof and physically stronger than humans. We also have better vision and hearing."

Some of the perks Andras had mentioned, no doubt.

"Because you showed such promise with the offensive art, I must warn you, if you feel yourself shuddering while you stand in place, change your thoughts immediately. But if you feel compelled to test your teleportation and accept the possibility of enduring painful catastrophe, then make sure to focus on exactly where you want to go.

Trust me, it's not fun to find yourself in the middle of an engine block." Heather chuckled.

"Andras wasn't kidding?"

"All demons can teleport and sense other demons, even through walls. But your aura ability gives you an even greater visual advantage. Practice switching on and off your demon vision and aura vision, so you don't end up with headaches from the visual noise. Your demon vision is what we all have—the ability to see other demons. They will appear to have a red cloudiness around them. Your aura vision, from what I've been told, will look, as you said, like shades of gray. Take some time to figure out your new self."

"I think I can handle that." I was, like, eighty-two percent certain I was going to wake up soon, completely baffled where a dream like this could originate from, and call my shrink.

After several turns in the brighter, but still dirty, hallway, my teacher stopped. Heather touched the dark stone wall, and the familiar bright blue phosphorescence returned. I grimaced at the bright light. She tapped an edge, and the door split open, revealing the shimmery portal.

Confused, I asked, "Don't you need a Hell badge to open that or something?"

Heather laughed. "Since I was born a demon, passage is encoded in my DNA. The magic that created you left behind its mark, and that mark will allow you passage. Don't be alarmed if you find something resembling a tattoo." I frowned, not wanting a mark on my perfect skin. "Andras File has a strange sense of humor."

Heather *Brush*, Andras *File*... "You have strange last names."

"Demons don't have last names. We just pick something when we must interact with humans to blend in."

They also had the creativity of a rock.

"Now remember," Heather said, "You must be careful. Master those skills. Control your thoughts. We don't need you accidentally starting an apocalypse."

"I'll try not to." I walked headfirst into the sparkly blue portal, planning to feed my fish right away. *Control*, I told myself, *remember control.*

16

Bad Demon

After feeding my fish, I scrubbed my skin raw in the hot shower for way longer than necessary. And there, over my heart, the tattoo I'd been warned about materialized right before my eyes. A circle first, followed by a second smaller circle inside of it. Then an inverted pentagram traced itself under my skin, and at the points, between the circle borders, symbols reminding me of old Norse appeared. I couldn't read what, if anything, the five symbols spelled. I waited, but nothing more appeared. Couldn't my first ink be something…cool? Why not a fire-breathing dragon? At least that would have some significance.

I scratched at it, but it was instantly healed and not going anywhere. I sighed, finished cleaning up, and re-styled my hair before hitting the elevator down. I strolled through my building, wearing my fancy demon-issued suit, grateful for the bright lights and clean tile. The floors were busy with work, and as I'd been warned, clouds in shades of gray hovered softly around each employee, but the density was more pronounced in their hearts. It was like peeking inside their heads, seeing the real person beneath the smiles and words.

I knocked on Jason Flick's door and pushed it open before waiting for a reply. The jittery and nervous accounting manager had a light gray cloud. The man was mostly good, but I wasn't sure if that information had value.

"Is there something I can do for you, boss?" he asked.

"No, just checking something. Continue on." I closed the door and went straight to Gary Levens's office. The finance manager's cloud was much darker. What did my own look like?

I excused myself and popped into the nearest employee restroom. In the mirror, my cloud wasn't a shade of gray at all. The heat swirling behind my eyes made my irises glow a brilliant red like Andras's had. I unbuttoned my shirt and tugged the fabric aside. There was the symbol. An employee pushed through the restroom door and was startled at seeing me. I shielded my face while the employee said, "Cool ink, boss. Did it hurt?"

"Uh, yeah, yes it did." Like having my insides burned to embers while I was alive.

"What do the symbols mean?"

"I'm not sure."

The employee leaned, trying to see my face. "Everything alright, boss? You don't usually come in here."

"I'm fine." My tone was sharper than I'd planned, but my employee shrugged and entered a stall.

I looked in the mirror again, and my irises continued glowing. What would happen if anyone saw this? I buttoned my shirt and focused on my serene fish, coasting through the turbulent saltwater waves, and my irises swirled back to their normal shade of blue. No wonder why Andras was always so cool and collected—he had to be.

I rode the elevator down to the ground level and followed the spinning doors onto the city sidewalk. A gust of autumn air ruffled my hair, but the chill didn't bother me. That was a nice benefit. Glancing up and down the sidewalk full of pedestrians, not one aura was pure white.

A young man smeared in filth with a torn knit hat, concert T-shirt, and holey jeans ran by me with a purse flailing behind him. The panicked man's aura was black. Moments later, a man's voice shouted above the crowd to stop the thief, but the perpetrator was long gone, swallowed by the sea of people.

There was no nightmare. There had been no hallucination. It was all real.

I needed to clear my head. I crossed the busy street, filled with honks and rumbling engines, and pushed through the door to the coffee shop. A blast of heady espresso and pumpkin spice filled my nose and cleared my sinuses. A television against the back wall babbled with the latest news, which sounded so petty now. What were human squabbles compared to the demons and angels lurking around us? I hadn't seen an angel yet, as far as I was aware, but just because I couldn't see them didn't mean they weren't around. Humans were blind, but I wasn't anymore.

A few customers sipped and talked, a few more typed on laptops. The line was thankfully short, and I stepped forward and ordered a satisfying nonfat cappuccino and waited. A familiar voice on the television turned my head. I smiled at the radiant blond—Shannon—from Channel 9 who'd interviewed me not long ago. The woman had flirted like men were going extinct. Not that I minded.

She talked about the release of a major new service, but I thought that was next week. I checked the date on the corner of the screen. That couldn't be right.

"Nick!" the barista called.

Following my name, I returned to the counter. "What day is it?"

"Thursday, the seventh."

I'd been gone half a week. What the hell happened in Hell? Andras had given me the rundown of the deal, sort of. The king showed up and chatted briefly. The witch performed an excruciating spell—if I could believe that was real, too. Then I woke up, got dressed, and played target practice with Heather. According to my watch—shit. It was melted. I sighed and paid. Something took far longer than the hour Andras promised, and the demon had been holding a massive knife when I woke up. Something happened. Something they kept from me.

The barista handed me the drink, and I accepted it, stuffing a tip in the jar. "Thanks."

I sipped the steamy brew and returned to the sidewalk. The gold and crimson leaves swirled at my feet, reminding me of a fire tornado. If I wanted to make a fire tornado, now I could. My livelihood, this glorious city of opportunity, this building and all of its valuable floors were important to me. I wouldn't want any of them destroyed. No, destroyed wouldn't do.

The corner of my lips lifted. I shook my head at how much had changed in only a few days. From my family and ex-girlfriend yelling at me for being such a screw-up—which made no sense—to being tortured in a demon dungeon, giving me the ability to wield fire and see people's true natures, like a window into their souls.

Heather Brush's insults floated back into my mind, followed by her promise to end me politically. Without legislative help on my side, keeping my business running would be challenging, if not impossible. But when she'd threatened to destroy my contract, I had exploded with rage.

Burning liquid splashed over my hand. Flames enveloped my fist and melted through the plastic cup. I flicked the hot coffee from my skin, but the fire held on for the ride. First her insults—did she believe them or were they strictly for training purposes?—and now my ruined drink.

Heather had said whatever was necessary to get a reaction from me, but what truly angered me about it was I believed her. That demon had spied on my company for...what had she said?...a year, three months, and six days. What else did that demon plan to destroy? The risk she placed upon my company infuriated me. A stream of fire shot from my palm, shifting me off balance with the sudden and unexpected force.

My mouth dropped open as the soaring spear of flame hit an elderly lady walking with a cane, knocking her off her feet. Passersby yelled for emergency services while onlookers hovered around her. The light gray aura clouding her chest floated up from her body and dissipated into the sky.

I stared. Did I do that?

My flame-free hand was scalded from the coffee, and the twisted plastic in my hand steamed.

"She's not breathing! Anyone know CPR?" a voice shouted above the ruckus.

I approached the woman, pushing my way through the growing audience. A smoking patch on her clothing was a giveaway. No one mentioned the bolt of fire or pointed me out as the culprit. With nothing I could do to help, I turned away. I should've cared. I should've been upset. I should've offered to pay for all her medical services. Every living person walking around had an aura cloud, but hers floated away from her body, so I knew she was dead. The witch's spell had twisted my consciousness and reduced my inhibition. For better or worse was yet to be determined, but I wasn't complaining, and I had other perks to explore.

I found an uninhabited alley around the corner. Juiced from the caffeine, I peeled off the cooled melted bits of plastic stuck to my hand and dropped them onto the ground. Next to the strewn garbage, overflowing dumpster—and judging by the ruffling noise—a rummaging cat (blergh), my littering hadn't added anything to the alley that wasn't already there.

At the far end was a chain-link fence—the perfect place to give this teleportation thing a whorl. I rubbed my hands together, shifted the weight on my feet, and closed my eyes, concentrating on moving without lifting a foot. A tugging on my body alarmed me, but no one was around. On the second try, I allowed the tugging to take me, while concentrating visually on the mark I wanted to land.

Within a moment, I shuddered in place, and when I opened my eyes, darkness surrounded me. With my new demon vision, shapes formed, and dread crawled down my spine. I wasn't caught in an engine block—it was much, much worse.

Inside the claustrophobic germy dumpster, a grating growl and the hiss of a cat startled me. I didn't like the furry creatures either, but damn, I didn't do anything to this one. The cat jumped out through an opening in the lid.

I tried to wade through the trash to climb out myself—ready to shower in bleach—but my feet wouldn't move. I turned on the flashlight feature of my cell phone and shined it at my ankles—or where they would be if the dumpster hadn't severed them at its raised floor.

Hot, searing pain radiated up my legs. I shoved the overhead lid open and concentrated on moving, but the pain demanded my attention. Bacteria crawling inside here, touching my legs, must've numbered in the billions. Tiny invisible critters snacking and defecating all over my skin, trying to invade my eyes and mouth. My heart thundered in its cage. My breaths quickened. Think, think, think, I told myself. Outside the dumpster. Feet on the asphalt. One, two, three...

I shuddered myself a few feet away. The pain instantly vanished. I brushed myself off and lifted my pant legs to check for damage. I couldn't imagine Heather's pain being trapped inside an engine block, but appears I survived my first ride unscathed. Extraordinary man's hair, impressive calves—if I said so myself—with no wounds or blood. But my shoes were gone. Twisting back toward the dumpster, I shined my flashlight under the base, and sure enough, my shoes rested where I left them.

Note to self: teleporting required concentration of not just where, but what. How was I going to get my shoes back? I wouldn't voluntarily return to the dumpster and sever my legs just to concentrate on my shoes. No way in hell was I walking bare socked across the alley.

I concentrated on moving just my shoes. I focused on the materials, the location, and visualized the shoes moving right next to my feet. Since they weren't attached, I couldn't feel the shudder, but when I thought enough time passed, I opened my eyes.

No shoes.

With a sigh, I tiptoed across the space, checking every square inch of asphalt before touching it. I kneeled with a cringe on a nearby piece of cardboard and reached under the dumpster.

On the list of the most disgusting things I'd ever done, that was right up there.

I slipped on my shoes, planning to clean them later, and exhaled in relief. Now I allowed the tugging to pull me again, but this time, I wanted to land back in my penthouse condo with my shoes. But at the last second, I thought of the woman I'd speared with fire.

The force delivered me to the sidewalk, where the woman was surrounded by emergency workers, and I knocked over a gawker. The crowd scowled at me.

"Get out of here, asshole," one man said. "You're in the way. What are you trying to do, pick her pockets? Goddamn homeless stinking up the place. You should be arrested for interfering with this woman's rescue."

My mouth dropped open, and I inspected my fireproof vicuña suit that probably cost more than the judgmental guy's car. I cringed at the trash bits and stains on the fabric. With irritation threatening to spark my hands, I returned to the alley, out of sight. If they were so harsh against a stinky businessman, what would they do if I were caught burning with no pain? And after the smoking hole in the elderly lady, how could I convince them my fire was harmless? Heather's warning about a cataclysmic event having caused angels and demons to agree to secrecy had me trusting her advice.

With all the dangers clear in my head, I tried to remember the benefits, because partially controllable fire and severed legs weren't part of it. Better vision, better hearing—seemed useless. Andras File made me a guarantee that sealed the deal for me: with this demonic power, I'd have no trouble with money. Andras didn't specify how, but I glanced at my palms. Remembering the accident with the old lady and the threat I'd previously given the banker—somehow what I had to do seemed...easy.

Threats were much more effective when they were real.

17

A Little Pressure

THE STREET GAWKER HAD heckled me for being filthy. To be ready to face Chuck Leach, I had to be shipshape. At home in my penthouse condo, I scrubbed and sterilized my shoes and, taking a chance my fancy threads would survive water, I ran my new suit through the wash. Then I hopped into the shower, and after lathering, rinsing, and repeating enough times to turn my skin red with irritation, I washed once more just to be sure. I had billions of bacteria to escape from, and the bottles didn't state the rate of bacteria elimination per lather. This was one of those emergency situations where it was far better to be safe than sorry.

While waiting for the dry cycle to complete, I visited my fish with a towel tied around my waist. "Hey, fellas. How's life treating you today?"

I sprinkled pellets across the surface and tossed in a couple cubes of frozen food. The fish went wild. After verifying that everyone was swimming well and free of signs of disease, I padded into the equipment room. The RODI water supply line was back to normal. My fish guy must've serviced the float switch, as asked. I shot him a text, thanking him and promising him a raise for the short notice. Only another fish guy would understand the strong sentiment I carried for my finned friends. Everyone else thought I was nuts—especially Chris.

The dryer cycle ended, and I dressed in warm, clean clothes, feeling like myself again. I teleported straight to the bank. Barging in on the man wouldn't earn me points, so I politely knocked on the banker's office door.

Chuck's muffled voice sounded like he was on the phone. I knocked again.

The mumbles ended, and the door opened. A dull, dark gray aura floated around the old man's body. Surprise to see me lifted his bushy brows. "Hey, kid. We don't have an appointment. What brings you here?"

I walked straight up to him, invading his personal space, and Chuck Leach backed up. Using that to my advantage, I closed the door behind us and blocked it. "Listen here, Chuck. I've played Nice Guy for a long time. I jumped through your little hoops to get my first loan. I kissed your ass for the subsequent—degrading myself to a beggar. What did it get me?"

Chuck Leach blinked, shock caging his tongue.

"Clarity," I finished for him.

Chuck backed up farther, shuffling toward his desk. "I've heard enough. This is my office. You don't barge in here uninvited and threaten me. Get out or you can consider our relationship over." The world-class poker face was gone. Guess all it took was shaking up his routine.

"Things are going to be different now." I stalked closer, purposely intimidating him. "You're going to give me that loan, and I won't kiss your ass or promise you anything. You know I'm good for it."

"I already told you there's nothing I can do."

"When you denied me, you said I could prove to you that was a mistake."

"I meant you could find a creative solution. Get out of here or I'm calling security." Chuck stared at me and puffed out his chest, but his own intimidation failed spectacularly. He was still stubborn as a mule, unfortunately for him.

I'd give the old man something to stare at. I centered my anger into my palm and flame enveloped my hand. After my visit to the restroom mirror, I recognized the sensation of painless heat in my irises triggering the unnatural red glow. A handy trick now. "Here's your proof."

"What in the Lord's name...?"

"God's got nothing to do with this." Or so I understood. Heather wasn't too clear on that.

"Wha...What's wrong with your eyes? Get out of my office!" Fear, not anger, raised Chuck's voice. He backed up until he fell into his chair. I casually sat in the customer chair, just where I'd been the last time. I squeezed my flaming hand, forming a short but deadly spear instead of a ball.

"I don't like my time wasted."

"I can't, Nick. I swear. They'll fire me. Please!" The loan officer held up his open palms in surrender.

"What do you think I'll do to you?"

To make my point, I released a warning flame at Chuck's mug, splashing coffee all over his desk and singeing the messy stacks of folders. Watching the stain-happy liquid roll toward me, I stood to protect my clothes.

The regrettable mess made me cringe, but sometimes sacrifices needed to be made.

Chuck rolled his chair away from the liquid but still within arm's reach of the phone. Sweat beads formed on his forehead, and he pushed his glasses back up his nose. "If you hurt me, no one will ever lend you a cent again. I'll blacklist you at every bank and credit union. I'll see to it! You can't get away with this."

I hardly tolerated the empty threats, but I wasn't going to allow the old man to destroy my future. I smirked and fisted another fireball and morphed it into a spear. A bigger one, just because. "What happens next is your choice, old friend. Remember that."

Chuck Leach glanced at the phone on his desk. After a moment's hesitation, he opened a drawer and set a towel over the spill. The banker wiped his hands dry on it and smeared the surface dry—inadequately sticky, but I picked my battles by letting that one go.

"I don't have all day here, Chuck. Will it be my papers or the phone?" I was running out of time, regardless. The tendrils of smoke from my fist were accumulating on the ceiling, minutes from triggering the fire alarm. Then I'd have too many witnesses.

The old man, who'd never shown emotion, teared up like a baby, a decision made. "Okay, okay. I'll do it. Just give me a minute?"

I smiled in satisfaction. "You made the right choice here, friend. You won't regret it."

The banker collected a pen from his holder and slipped a stack of papers out of a drawer. He turned them over and scrawled large letters across the white sheets. After a telltale glance at me, he lifted the handset.

"You're making me do this," I reminded him. Without another second's chance, I shot the flaming spear straight into Chuck's chest, throwing him back against the chair, and stopping his fingers before they depressed a number. The handset fell out of his hand, and the cord's tension pulled it against the desk with a bang. The wound instantly cauterized, but it sizzled like bacon, and the singed fabric glowed. "This path...will be...your end."

I stood and leaned over the desk, holding my tie away from the sticky mess, and turned Chuck's last words around. "I'm pretty sure it's *your* end."

Chuck's vacant eyes stared at the ceiling as if his last thoughts were begging his soul to remain. His dark gray aura drifted up, blending into the smoke, and then disappeared through the ceiling like a ghost. White meant pure, Andras had said, and black meant evil, but all the shades of gray were players in the game. I figured out the shades meant levels of morality.

No need to check for a pulse. I liked Chuck, so I tilted the old man until his head rested on his desk in a peaceful pose. What kind of man traded his life for money—for the bank's money?

Frustrated with the outcome, I inspected myself for flames before teleporting back to my building, because A—I didn't want to cause a panic, but mostly B—I didn't want to burn down the one thing I'd put my life into. Even if I only caught a few floors on fire, and even if my insurance covered the damage, weeks could pass before payment was received and work began. So much lost time, and I didn't have any more to spare.

The fire alarm overhead triggered. My heart jumped into my throat. Time to get the hell out of here. I focused my thoughts, directing my whole body—shoes included—to the sidewalk, just to be safe. The wailing scream tore into my concentration. Footsteps thundered down the hall outside the door. The office doorknob clicked as someone attempted to enter.

I had to get out of here now.

I inhaled deeply and coughed. I exhaled slowly and focused again. Sidewalk. Cool breeze. Fresh air. Sidewalk, I repeated. The door squeaked as my shudder dragged me away. Shades of autumn dotting the street flickered like gems in the sunlight. Pedestrians filled the downtown sidewalk, and their coats fluttered in the breeze. I bumped into people who hadn't seen me and received a few ugly glares. I checked my hands, and they were fire-free. So far, so good.

Clouds of gray from the human auras covered the sidewalks like a blanket of morning fog, but this wasn't a weather event. It was only a sea of people with their souls on display for me.

I concentrated on turning off the aura vision. Not because I didn't like it, no, having that kind of information was interesting if not useful, but because the density of clouds muddied up the beautiful scenery. Like an algae infestation on my coral, I only wanted to see it when I needed it. I focused on seeing the humans as they were, and a strong tension overtook my body. Instantly, I stopped that one. No need to teleport somewhere randomly. I shifted the focus somewhere else until I found just the right trigger to flip in my head. After straining a groin muscle, trying to turn it off, the clouds around the people vanished like a light switch.

I shook out my leg. I was going to need gym time to loosen that up.

Behind me, a woman's lungs rattled with a deep cough, as if she were at the end of a long battle with pneumonia. With her arms full of shopping bags, nose bright from tissue irritation, and eyes drawn with exhaustion, coughs seized her again. Passersby gave her a wide berth to avoid contamination. I covered my mouth with my tie to filter the air I breathed.

That was the answer.

18

The New Plan

TELEPORTING WAS MY FAVORITE ability, and it was handy as hell. But after that public incident with the old lady and now Chuck Leach, I had to be more careful. More discreet. People—both my employees and the public at large—couldn't witness my glowing red eyes, flaming basketballs or spears, and my vanishing in the blink of an eye. I had every intention of continuing to enjoy my gifts, but I wanted to return to my normal life and maintain my trustworthy image. Although I didn't remember the details of the spell, all that mattered were the results.

And I was getting results right now.

Using my splayed palm to open the lab's anteroom, I entered and gowned up. I might never need hand sanitizer again, but I wouldn't risk getting infected by all the other creepy crawlies in the lab. Doors parting, I inhaled the relaxing scent of antiseptic and lemons, so much more effective than a bottle of Dennis's beer or my rum and Coke. Easier on the waistline, too.

Dr. Tyler Gibson's white marshmallow suit crinkled when he lifted his head from the microscope. "Hey, boss. I didn't hear the anteroom open. What brings you down here? It's good news, I hope."

I marched down the aisle—as manly as a man sporting an oversize marshmallow suit, white booties, and a light blue hairnet could—and I approached my microbiologist. "I have answers."

Gibson beamed and rose, distracting glasses tilted behind his mask. He scrunched his nose and aligned them. "When does the new staff begin? Can I meet them? Give them the tour?" He leaned around me as if expecting them to have followed.

"I couldn't get you any employees."

Gibson's smile dropped behind his mask. "I understand it takes time to find them, but we're on a deadline here." He tapped his wrist where a watch would be. "The first shipment is getting closer and closer to impossible by the day. At this rate, there's likely no chance we will make that deadline."

On a deadline here... That hadn't changed.

Closer to impossible... I could feel this with every breath.

No chance... This was alarming.

My new plan was still going to take time to notice the results, but it would work. I needed something else to make my plan succeed. One missing step. I smiled, but the microbiologist couldn't see it behind my mask. "Don't lose hope yet, Gibson. Change in plan. I need you to stop producing The Annihilator."

Dr. Gibson frowned. "I said it was close to impossible. You're throwing in the towel completely? All this work down the drain?"

"Our problem is time. It always was, but now I figured out a way to twist the time in our favor. Send the formula for Heromycin up to the plant immediately. I need large-scale doses available for the public within weeks."

Dr. Gibson cocked his head as if still not understanding. "To accomplish that feat—without more staff—we'd have to drop Anycillin from production entirely. You want to cut our flagship product?"

"Are you questioning my strategy?" I kept my mind calm, so my best geek didn't get a full view of the red glow.

"I'm the lab rat. You're the boss." Gibson shrugged.

"There's a reason I keep you around." I appreciated accolades whenever and wherever they came from.

"So, it's not for my pretty face?" Dr. Gibson tilted his head, teasing me.

I enjoyed my colleague's banter, a respite from my new roller-coaster anger, so I played along. "I haven't seen you without a mask in so long, I don't remember what you look like."

"You'll have to take me out some night to remind yourself. I'm a cheap date."

"I don't think your wife will appreciate that."

"Nah, you're right. She'd be jealous."

I chuckled. "Focus, Gibson. We have work to do." I gestured to move around Gibson toward the clear vault, but the microbiologist stood and held out his hands, stopping me.

Dr. Gibson cleared his throat, returning to business. "I do have one question, if you don't mind. According to the research and the schedule, we won't need to mass produce Heromycin for a year. So if we make it now, its short shelf life means it'll go to waste. What good is the antibiotic spoiling on a shelf if the government doesn't get the bacteria first?"

"Like I said, I have a new plan." I swerved around the lab manager and beelined for the clear vault. Two Annihilators, I believed in redundancy, and one Heromycin, the second of which was supposed to be finished soon. The test tubes sat in a clear rack behind several sheets of locked and bulletproof acrylic. I considered wrapping my knuckles and punching through it to test my new strength, but I decided against causing unnecessary repairs to the lab with so much work ahead of us. My knuckles were likely to become dust against that acrylic, anyway. The enclosure was too small to teleport inside, unless I wanted a repeat of the dumpster mishap, only with all my limbs and neck this time. I sighed. No special abilities for this situation. "Gibson! Key. Where's the key?"

"What for, boss?"

I beckoned the lab manager with the curl of my finger. Gibson set down a stack of folders and closed the distance, swishing with his puffy marshmallow suit. I said, "I need a test tube of The Annihilator."

Gibson frowned. It wasn't protocol, but sometimes rules needed to be broken. "What are you going to do with it?" he asked slowly, as if worried about my new interest in the deadly bacteria.

"That's not your concern. Keys, Gibson." I crooked my fingers again.

"Nick, this is my work. You're paying for my skill in creating this dangerous weapon, so it's my responsibility to see it's handled appropriately. You barging in here—"

"Me barging?" I interrupted. My fists balled, but I recalled Heather's advice—*Controlling your emotions means choosing which voice in your head to listen to. Take a moment to process and make sure you choose wisely.* My lab manager's aura had been obscured through the puffy white suit, and it was so close to white, it was barely perceptible. Dr. Gibson was, indeed, good people—whip smart and impossible to replace. I focused on my geek's crooked glasses. I wanted to fix them. The man deserved to be able to see properly. But I couldn't allow him to see properly. He could never see the real me. The man had no clue what I was or what else was hiding in plain sight. I needed to break the glasses. I wanted to. And now, he was standing between me and what mattered most.

I felt the swirl behind my eyes, and I closed them. I wanted to tear this lab apart to get my hands on that test tube. It would be easy, and I presume much fun, but I focused on the sharp scent of lemons. *Think, think, think. Choose the right voice.*

If I gave in to the desire to rip Gibson out of my way, what would happen? I couldn't get warm bodies with brains in here. How would I ever replace the one scientist the CDC wanted but couldn't have? Gibson was mine. He was important. I needed *him* most of all.

I was too close to let my thoughts destroy everything. *Control*, I told myself, *remember control.* I brought up images of my fish cavorting and the anemones swaying in the wave makers. The desire to unleash this festering fury eased.

Gibson still stepped back. "I just mean that you being in here is already compromising the safety and integrity of the lab, and I'm very concerned about what you plan to do with the sample. Are you giving it to the competition to make? Level with me if you are. You owe me that much."

Calm fully returned, I gazed at my best employee. "I appreciate your concern, but you can trust me. I built this company with my own metaphorical hands. This is just one more bullet point in the job description." I tossed in a sweet smile for good measure—mostly covered, but still, the point reached home.

A puffy arm surrendered the metal ring of keys. "Be careful. If these bacteria were released, it would have catastrophic effects. The things I saw infected mice doing—it wasn't right."

First, I would never go anywhere near the mice. Second, that was interesting. I accepted the keys and asked, "What were they doing?"

"From the data we've collected so far, the mice appear to first develop a wet cough. It doesn't present the same as in humans, so it was tricky to find. Larger test subjects would've made the process quicker, but I worked with what we had. After various lengths of incubation, and after testing with every available antibiotic at every dose feasible, most of the subjects died."

"That's what the government ordered. What's the problem?"

Gibson cringed. "A few of the subjects came back to life."

Huh. It wasn't every day someone actually surprised me. "You're sure they were dead to begin with?"

"Mice have different physiological responses than humans, and I'm not a veterinarian, but I'm completely certain all their organs and circulatory system ceased to function, but after various lengths of time, the brain restarted electrical activity on its own."

"Is that bad?"

"The other organs and circulation didn't restart."

That sounded bad.

"I don't like this, boss, but it's your company. I'm just glad we have Heromycin." Gibson returned to his work, and I unlocked the vault. Of the two Annihilator tubes on standby, I removed one.

On my way to the anteroom, I tossed the keys back to my favorite geek. "You're doing good work here. Keep it up."

Gibson gestured in response but didn't lift his eyes from the paperwork. Yep, good people, even if a little pissed.

I tore off the ridiculous lab-wear and pocketed a fresh pair of nitrile gloves—insufficient for the task at hand, but I could burn the bacteria off my body, even if it revolted me. Besides, I wouldn't get away with the full HAZMAT outfit I'd rather wear. People tended to freak when someone showed up wearing full body protection at the food court. Well, this time they should.

SECURITY AT POLITICAL RALLIES was too tight. The next state fair wouldn't be around until summer. I needed a populated place. Most areas of the country had seen a vast decline in mall traffic from its peak, especially in smaller cities, and the trends suggested that heyday would never return. Luckily for me, there remained one in a busy area downtown, near the NBB building.

Shoppers murmured above the slurps, gulps, and crunches of their meals. Cell phones chirped with texts. Teenage girls giggled and posed for selfies. Apparently, my hearing improved with my vision—a benefit Heather had told me about. But the ability to see chewed bits flying with peals of laughter and the gristle trapped between teeth were not benefits. Turning my eyes away before my stomach flipped, I closed my lids and focused on the eateries' sizzling, and a heavenly scent of burgers and pizza filled my nose. Hey, everyone deserved a cheat day once in a while.

All around me were families, friends, and acquaintances having their fun, taking a break from shopping, or just meeting up for an afternoon's browsing. I heard there was an escape room nearby—a big hit with the twenty-somethings. So many people, so innocent and oblivious.

Sitting at the back corner of the food court, somehow not flattening the table with his immense rear, Odie the elephant watched in silence. His face displayed clear disapproval—beyond the trunk. Some friend he was. Frowning, I attempted to ignore the elephant in the room, but it wasn't like him to disapprove of me. I studied the shiny green liquid filling the test tube in my gloved palm.

I could still put it back, find another way, and I wanted to. I wanted to fulfill the contract by delivering the product, collecting my checks, and then swoop in to the rescue with Heromycin. But I couldn't. I'd tried everything I could, but as Dr. Gibson said, *there's likely no chance we will make that deadline.* And he was a brilliant man.

I'd promised the CDC and the DoD I would meet the terms. So not only was I on track to lose the contract, but my reputation would be shot, and any possibility of future business together hung in the balance.

If I didn't do this, the government would find someone else to make the bacteria. The only realistic possibility was my competition, Ted Bastard. His company, Novalite Pharmaceuticals, if it were smart enough—and I hated to give Ted the benefit of the doubt, but I did—would create its own bacterium from scratch and an antibiotic to counter it, leaving my Heromycin ineffective and Anycillin useless. I would be ruined. I'd have to crawl back to my parents and apologize for not listening, but I'd rather visit that glitter-covered, unicorn-haired, skewer-wielding dude in Hell. Then I'd have to sell the NBB building before the carrying cost sunk me. I'd be lucky to find a decent apartment in the city, and not only would I have to let my fish guy go, but what would I do with a twenty-foot-long aquarium? Where would my fish and corals go? The shame and embarrassment were too much to imagine, and even worse, I'd be heartbroken. If I chickened out now, my life would be over. Everything I built, destroyed.

I uncorked the tube.

Odie's disapproving glare turned into a thin-lipped scowl. *I'm not your entertainment,* I silently chastised. *If you don't have any answers, leave me alone!* The elephant didn't move. It didn't say anything, and it wouldn't leave. Of course not. I turned my back on it.

What I was about to do would anger the government for overstepping. They might even consider prison time, but with mass panic, they'd be forced to turn to me for the rescue, and at that point, I would renegotiate. In exchange for a new contract—with my own reasonable deadline, Gibson would modify the redundant sample into a new strain. The government would get what it ultimately wanted, just late. I would keep my reputation as someone capable, who kept his word, and I would be the world's hero, just as I ultimately wanted. This was fully win-win, and Heather would be proud that I considered both voices in depth, and I'd chosen the right one to listen to.

I glanced across the food court one last time. Odie was gone. Perhaps I'd finally conquered my imaginary friend. Control wasn't that hard.

With a quick smirk of victory, I muttered to myself, "Sometimes the only way to save the world is to destroy it first."

I dunked a gloved finger inside the test tube with a cringe—I'd toast any residual germs from my hands immediately after this nightmare-inducing Hail Mary pass. With the deadly creepy crawlers swarming my fingers, I squeezed between seated customers, purposely bumping into them and touching their arms and shoulders. Whenever the opportunity showed itself, I smeared my fingers on chair backs and tabletops. I bumped into a man walking by with a tray of food.

"Hey, watch where you're going, buddy," the portly fellow in a ball cap said and scowled.

I smiled, genuinely friendly, since I finally had the solution. "I'm so sorry. I just had a rough day, and I got lost in my thoughts. Can I give you a hand?"

"What? No!" The man shifted his tray away from my grasp.

I continued more discreetly until I believed the whole food court was infected, and I ran out of bacteria to share. I inverted the gloves while removing them to protect myself and tossed them and the empty into the trash on my way out. Satisfied with a job well done, I teleported home for a shower and a bacteria-killing burn on my hands. Success was within my grasp. I hoped I was careful enough to avoid the sickness myself.

19

Disappointed

THE GYM UNDER MY penthouse condo was empty, as expected. The evenings were my private time, unless Andras wanted to join me. My feet pummeled the treadmill's belt while I watched the pre-game chatter. The rubbery stench of mats and the metallic taste in my mouth from the equipment was a warm welcome after the nightmare visit to Hell and the germ-fest at the mall. So far, I felt fine, even after overly exerting myself. So fine, in fact, I definitely had more stamina than before, and I wasn't even sweating.

The familiar clatter of the front door pulled the corners of my lips. Speak of the lizard... "Hey, Andras, just on time for the game."

Andras strolled over in his tank top and baggy athletic shorts and flung a towel over the digital screen, giving me only a glance and no usual greeting. If I didn't know better, I could swear there was a hint of disappointment on my friend's face.

"Talk to me. What's up?"

The cranky demon pressed buttons on the treadmill's console. Andras kept pace with me, and we both watched the game. When the commercial hit, Andras finally asked, "How are you adjusting?"

"I haven't burned anything by accident lately." Only on purpose.

"Is that so?"

"Yep. Control's not so hard when you find a focus. Why didn't you tell me what this was from the beginning?" If I'd had these abilities sooner, I might've been able to salvage my contract without having to infect the world, not that I was blaming my friend.

"Convincing you to join the team was risky even before I met you. So you'll understand how I addressed the situation with extreme caution."

"Team? What team? Why do I feel pertinent information is being withheld on purpose? After spending how long with a scary blond behemoth, who turned me into this, you need to level with me, because I'm not returning anything for a refund."

Andras cracked a smile. "There are no refunds in Hell. A team is a group of Field Agents. Remember the miles of cubicles in Hell?"

How could I forget? After encountering the man decked in glitter with unicorn-colored hair and wielding a barbecue skewer, the endless cubicles were the only semblance of normal I'd noted down there. "I remember."

"Those are Desk Agents. Most of them wish to be promoted to Field Agent. Mingling with humans is more exciting than a desk job."

I couldn't argue with that. "Your job titles are lacking in creativity."

"That's what I said."

The audience on the television cheered the new leader at the end of the third quarter. My treadmill shifted its incline and finally, sweat rolled down my body. My calves burned wonderfully. I'd become one of them, but I had no idea what that entailed. "What do the Field Agents, we, do? Because, if it involves managing humans, you couldn't have picked a better guy."

"You're not a Field Agent yet. We're giving you a chance to figure yourself out, so when the time comes, you'll be as efficient and careful as we need you to be. By now you've seen the human auras. The white ones we ignore. They're too hard to budge, and therefore, a waste of time. The black auras are already set to go and not worth further attention. Field Agents' job, which we've been doing blindly for a while, is to make the auras darker by influencing their actions to tip the balance."

I snorted. "You want to corrupt humans? I can't say I'm surprised. All this power's going to waste. We'd own all the wealth in this country. Control the top industries globally. I want to buy a ski cabin in Colorado, a vacation home in the Florida Keys—er, well, not so much anymore, and..." I considered my next splurge after impending revenues soared. I'd spent years building the corporate ladder, so I'd never taken a real vacation. "I think I'll have a yacht custom-designed for deep sea fishing adventures in the Keys—or women and booze. You're invited." I smiled.

Andras wasn't amused. "I heard about what happened to Chuck Leach."

"That's why you're cranky with me? I was discreet about it."

"A hole was burned through his chest. What's discreet about that? Nick, we can't let the public find out about what we are. Mass panic and rioting would harm us more than help."

Andras's defeatist attitude was baffling.

"If we cause a panic, doesn't that help your cause?" What better way to corrupt humans than to bring out their baser instincts?

"*Our* cause," Andras corrected and pressed a button on the console. The treadmill slowed to a stop. Andras mopped his face but hardly panted at all. Now I understood his amazing strength and endurance. Counting macros? That was a load of bull, but Andras had never been juicing, either. He just squeezed a giant, purple-scaled, shiny, iridescent lizard-demon into a passable human form.

I ended my twelve-mile jog and sat next to my friend on the weight bench. I slammed down a bottle of water and never felt better. We watched the game nearing its end, and Andras said, "A few people with an easy agenda can influence many. If the demons cause a mass panic, where do you think the vast majority of humans will turn?"

I supposed people usually turned to their leadership for answers and guidance. Under the wrong influence, I supposed that could be dangerous. "Are you saying the elected officials are angels?"

Andras snorted and laughed for the first time all night. "As part of the secrecy pact, demons and angels have vowed to remain outside of human laws. Churches are another story. When was the last time you saw a temple worshiping demons?"

"Never? But they exist."

"Far, far fewer than those dedicated to the light, which go back thousands of years. Worshiping the dark openly is a fairly new construct. The simple truth is we are outnumbered by both the angels and the humans. This is about survival and nothing more."

"If the Good Book is entirely fiction, and Hell tortures people instead of souls, and witches exist, and demons and angels are tangible beings..." I trailed off, trying to make sense of the world around me.

"Go on."

"Where do you—I mean, angels and demons—come from?"

Andras sighed. "I suppose that information wouldn't be harmful for you to know. According to our demon history, we were brought here. Think of it like a Noah's Ark thing. A group of angels, a group of demons, and a group of humans. And like all mixed societies, the squabbling started immediately. Groups broke into their respectful cultures, and a battle for power began. The story is as old as time."

The answer made me laugh. "You're aliens?"

Andras frowned. "All of us came here together. I'm no more an alien than you are, than the President of the United States, than little Timmy in the hospital. We are all equals except for some biological differences."

"You mean these amazing powers?" I grinned.

"Nick, I'm only going to say this once. If you refuse the rules of the supernatural world, there are consequences."

"Heather already gave me the speech." My anger festered. "And her delivery was better."

"But still you didn't listen."

Well, Chuck deserved what he got, but after hearing the tale and seeing what could happen, that I could agree with. "I'll be more careful."

"Good. And realize the king is coming for you. We have a job to do."

That I wouldn't agree with. "I already have a job, and I'm not quitting to work for anyone else—not even the king." Especially not a king. I could imagine his pompous demands and ridiculous customs. I was done taking orders from anyone. "You didn't disclose all the facts prior to that witch's spell, so that's on you. Besides, I haven't seen whatever the 'partnership for a fun and easy life' is about. Consider it a breach of contract. And you said Hell had no refunds."

With the final cheers on the screen, Andras said, "Your team lost."

The big man stood up and walked out with his head hung low. There was the disappointment I was so used to seeing, but this time, it didn't sting so much.

No longer interested in pumping iron, I turned off the television. I wasn't a joiner—never was, never would be. Demons had more power than any human ever dreamed of, but they only used it to secretly herd humans around like cattle. I didn't know where angels fit in here, but all I understood was they weren't friendly.

That wasn't my business. I had bigger fish to fry—I hated that phrase—like controlling the world's antibiotic trade. Any day now, a supply would be ready for the historical demand I had created. By Andras's warning, it appeared Hell was nervous about me.

As *they should be.*

20

So It Begins

I FINISHED SENDING AN email when my stomach growled. Since my watch had melted, I checked the clock on my office computer monitor. There had to be a reimbursement expense form somewhere in Hell. Damage was done while on the clock—so to speak.

If I was desperate, I'd hit up the cafeteria, but this morning I put in a takeout request with my assistant. Noon had already passed, but Chelsea was nowhere in sight, and no one could sneak by my office without being noticed. I lifted the handset from my desk phone to remind her, when my door opened, but it wasn't Chelsea.

Chris walked in, more pale than usual. Since Chris's blow up on the phone over his marketing plan being placed on hold, we hadn't spoken. And since I couldn't get a loan from Chuck Leach, I forgot to give my big brother the bad news. Actually, we never really spoke much at all on principle. I suppose I could hand down the bad news now, but obviously he wanted something, and he wasn't angry yet.

"What can I do for you?" I asked coolly.

"Have you seen the news?" Chris closed the door behind him and coughed into his fist.

"Not lately. Did you see Chelsea on your way in?" I wanted my lunch more than anything right now.

My brother frowned and took a seat, uninvited. Chris's brow beaded with sweat and his skin was pallid, almost like a translucent sheen wrapped around him. This was something more than just nerves.

"No, I didn't. She probably called in sick, just like a quarter of the city."

It didn't take a whiz to figure out what was happening, and I shouldn't be surprised at the level of genius in Dr. Gibson, but, frankly, I was impressed. And utterly, genuinely horrified. I might be a demon, but I wasn't a monster.

My single test tube of bacteria was too potent if it sickened that many people already. The lab wasn't finished changing over the lines to Heromycin, and Production hadn't received enough raw material stock to begin. (For once, I wish I didn't fire Heather). And I knew because I approved all major purchases, and none passed my desk lately. Unless... I rose.

"Where are you going?"

"I need to check something." No reason to panic, yet.

I popped out of my office and strolled down the hallway. Chelsea's desk was missing her pretty face. I skimmed the documents on the surface, looking for a purchase order, and there it was. I eagerly grabbed a pen, signed it, and tracked down the first person who looked like they knew how to run these machines.

"Nadia, scan this to my email, please."

The woman stopped short in her tracks, looked at the document with a raised brow, and said, "Sure, boss." She brought it behind Chelsea's desk and worked her magic with the buttons. When she finished, she handed me the paper. "You're all set."

"Thank you. You're a lifesaver."

She cocked her head and continued on her way. Straightening my tie, I headed back into my office and parked my rear in my chair. I opened my email, found the file, and forwarded that off to the supplier.

Because I knew how Chris would react if he knew my hand in this, I played dumb. "Sorry about the interruption. What's the sickness you were talking about?"

"Turn on the local news, and you'll see."

I switched on the television, and the news anchor, Shannon, had a doctor on a split screen. There was a distinct lack of flirting going on—not that it was important, just noteworthy.

"Local internal medicine specialist, Dr. Brenner, joins us today to explain his recommendations about this alarming new sickness taking over the city. Dr. Brenner?"

With a small frown at the news anchor's choice of words, the doctor said, "Thank you, Shannon. Although no available antibiotics appear effective, we are working diligently to find answers to this unprecedented bacterial spread. I can assure the public that although Mercy's laboratory confirmed unusual characteristics of this bacterium, the reports calling it a plague and an apocalypse are inaccurate, and they should be ashamed of themselves for causing unnecessary concern. Mercy Medical Center urges residents of the city to continue hand washing, avoiding crowds, and to stay home whenever possible. At this point, we suspect the illness only needs time to work its way through the population, but please be safe until a treatment can be found."

"A harrowing rumor flying out of control. Thank you, doctor, for straightening that out. More tonight at nine."

"A little scary, don't you think?" Chris asked.

I switched off the television. Their panic would only continue compounding, because there was nothing for them to do. I had the only cure. For now, it was only two doses, but the rest would be available in no time. My lips tugged into a small, satisfied smile.

"What are you so happy about?"

My plan wasn't a complete disaster. "I think it's a great opportunity."

"Great opportunity?" Chris's upper lip curled in disgust. "People are getting sick in a scary pattern, and doctors are prescribing Anycillin, since they don't know what else to do, but Anycillin's on backorder. Shortages are causing a panic, never mind it doesn't work. I dug around, Nick, because I know you want nothing more than money and fame, so for you to order Anycillin production to shut down, you have something up your sleeve for this. But development and testing take time, and the approval process is lengthy—even on an emergency basis. For someone who's profit-minded, shutting down Anycillin wasn't a good move. Why?"

My brother didn't understand, and that was one of the key differences between us—why one was the employee and the other the employer.

"What if I told you we have the cure?"

Chris squinted as the wheels turned. He stood and rubbed a hand over his short hair. I knew that face—the symbolic light bulb, the moment Chris figured out the truth for himself. "Oh, no, no, no. No, I can't believe this. How could you? How did you?"

"It's not what you think."

Big brother paced the office, jabbing a finger at me to make his points. "You did this! You developed this catastrophic disease in secret, didn't you? This whole 'extra money for miscellaneous expenses' thing was a ruse. I smelled it a mile away. How else could a multi-million-dollar company be so broke it can't afford a marketing campaign or hire a few employees? Because you're secretly pouring millions into research and development."

Close enough, but I knew better than to interrupt one of my brother's rants. I wanted my face to retain its handsome shape.

"I'm not surprised! Actually, you know what? You want my honest opinion?"

No, but I guessed it was coming, anyway.

"I'm disgusted you're my brother. Always have been. Everything we've done to help you be a better person was a waste. How are we even related?" Chris bent to cough as if his rant sucked the air from his lungs. '*Tis the season*. While the man was occupied with regaining his composure, I covered my own mouth with my tie.

Dryly, I said, "I'm glad you're taking this all personally and felt the need to hit below the belt. What else are families for?"

Chris continued coughing, but the hatred in his eyes spoke volumes. When he settled, Chris silently stewed, waiting for more explanation.

"They're called The Annihilator and Heromycin, if you want to put names to the acting agents, and I didn't do it to harm anyone. Believe it or not, NBB has a contract." Secret was all over the news. I was only explaining my side to smooth over my family drama.

Chris glared. "*The Annihilator*? Please give me one good reason for all this. Maybe you'll be redeemed in Mother's eyes."

Despite not giving a damn what Stella Barnes thought any longer, I cringed at the look on my brother's face, so I offered him something for peace of mind. "The government paid me to create a new strain of bacteria for their own use, the details of which I wasn't given. As a businessman who cares about people, I also developed the antibiotic to cure it—*that* they don't know about."

"Are you saying the government released your bioweapon on us?" The look of horror on Chris's face pained me, because it wasn't them, and I hadn't *wanted* to do it.

"I wouldn't call my bacteria a bioweapon. It just causes sickness." And widespread death and several cases of reanimation in mice, according to Dr. Gibson. But those details wouldn't help my case. Besides, people weren't mice. (Thank God—er, aliens? And I forgot to ask Andras where those tiny hellbeasts originated, so I could send someone a very strongly worded letter about the appropriateness of such evil in a tiny body, and to please remove them from the earth, much appreciated.)

"That said," I continued, "in order for you to have your marketing campaign and for me to afford the staff I needed, I had to take drastic measures." I didn't count on it being so successful.

"I don't understand any of this. I gave you a plan to increase revenue. The pamphlets, remember?" How could I forget that stupid suggestion? "And you fired Heather Brush. Didn't that help?"

"Not really, no, but I'm going to approve your ad campaign, if you can adjust it from Anycillin to Heromycin."

"With what money?"

I was going to ask him to personally fund it or ask him to negotiate extensions on the accounts payables for those vendors, or extend our credit with them, but at this point, if Chris had demon eyes, they'd be flaring something fierce right now, so I didn't say anything.

Chris leaned against my desk, getting in my face. I backed up from his germs. "If anyone dies from this, it's all on your head."

"No one is going to die." Probably because Gibson's bacterium was supposed to be fatal, but it hadn't been tested on humans, and now it didn't matter. "And everyone is going to be praising me for saving them all. You'll see." My smugness was dying to spill my secret demon curse. Perhaps if I introduced Chris to the hidden world around us with my glowing eyes and flaming hands, maybe he'd change his opinion—or at least his tone. But with Chris's scowling hatred... No, he wasn't ready yet.

"You think this is funny? Dad was wrong. Dad was actually wrong." Chris raked a hand over his trimmed hair.

Interest piqued, I leaned forward. "Go on."

"You're not a failure. Not one bit. Congratulations, Nick! You'll go down in history as the world's greatest mass murderer."

That wasn't the compliment I'd hoped for. And I bet that wasn't accurate, either, but I didn't have numbers to defend myself, and Chris wasn't in the mood to argue semantics. I raised my brows and reminded myself of my fish, so I didn't accidentally flash Chris my red angries.

"I'm...I'm done here. I'm taking a personal leave. Don't call me." Chris turned away.

"When you're ready to get back to work, I'll be here. There's plenty to be done."

Chris paused with his hand on the knob, considering my statement for a moment. He opened the door and slammed it shut behind himself without another word. He'd come around, eventually. Chris still needed a paycheck.

In the meantime, I rode the elevator down to the underground lab and gowned up in a full marshmallow suit. The microbiologist wasn't in sight. Probably in the restroom. Curiosity getting the better of me and patience not being one of my virtues, I paged through the reports left near the microscope. None of the geeks paid me any attention or interrupted me. Good. They had urgent work to do.

Among the papers were labor forecasts and FDA approval timelines ready to go but not processed. Dr. Gibson was one on-the-ball dude, but where was he? Well, I didn't have time for Gibson to finish his morning business. I found a scrap of paper and a pen and scribbled a note to my favorite geek to rush the process, since demand was expected to be staggering and sooner than planned. "But the demons were going to be happy about this," I muttered to myself.

Priority one was now securing the purchase of raw materials above all others. Small potatoes, probably.

21

Mashed Potatoes

A CHUNK OF THE city was sick already, and only a few days had gone by. That sounded great at first, but if the public fought off the sickness before Heromycin reached the market, then releasing the bacteria in the first place would've been for nothing. I refused to entertain that dreadful thought.

What I could do was check my email for the verification receipt of the raw materials order, but I found something far more urgent. From the office of the CDC, a letter.

Dear Mr. Nick Barnes,   We want to inform you that while we looked forward to the delivery of your first shipment, we received startling news. Medical providers have shipped a sample of an illness spreading through your city, and after studying it, we can confirm, without a doubt, it matches the deadly sample you developed for us.   The safety of the public is our number one priority, so you can imagine our concern. We want to give you the benefit of the doubt on how such a catastrophe could've happened, and with that in mind, we hope you've taken the initiative to craft an antibiotic.   However, since our contract was for a new bacterium for our purposes, we regret to inform you that its release nullifies the contract, but considering the circumstances, we won't impose a fine or have the Attorneys General press charges, due to the sensitivity of this project.   Please update us the moment you have an antibiotic capable of destroying this bacterium.   Sincerely,   Drs. Branston and Rhee Centers for Disease Control and Preventionundefined

My contract was gone. I'd expected that, but I also expected if I could pull through on the antibiotic, the CDC and I would be back in business. Because I was capable of making such a thing, they needed me to unmake it. Likely that was the real reason for backing away from their threat. But they sounded worried. The CDC was all the way on the other side of the country. Was my bacterium *that* good?

I didn't see a receipt confirmation from the purchase order I'd signed and emailed over, so I called our cellulose supplier directly.

The vendor's voice was surprisingly friendly. "You've been a reliable customer of ours for years, and I'm hoping Anycillin is going to lick that problem over there. Every manufacturer is hounding me for their orders in hopes of capitalizing on this new sickness, but I will personally make sure you receive priority service."

Good man. "I appreciate it."

A computer mouse clicked several times over the phone, and that cheeriness faltered. "According to the database here, the last invoice we sent you was never paid. We've been in contact with your accounts payable rep, but we're getting the runaround on a payment date. I can't authorize another shipment until this invoice is cleared. I'm sorry, Mr. Barnes."

Heather Brush's unusually high order of cellulose had been an attempt to stave off a shortage affecting production. We'd used it up on the useless Anycillin before it expired. And now the increased demand I'd caused led to a shortage, and that order of materials still hadn't been paid for. The string of bad luck was frustrating. I grumbled under my breath and scribbled a note for Jason Flick to get on it at once—no matter where he had to scrape the funds from. "We'll get you paid. You get me that material."

A knock on my door had me hanging up the phone.

Chelsea walked in, but it wasn't lunchtime. Hopefully, it wasn't more bad news. "What can I do for you, Chelsea?"

My assistant paused at the threshold to cough into her elbow, and I held out my hand sanitizer. She took a pump and passed me a note.

"What's this?"

"A Tyler Gibson wants you to call him." Chelsea coughed again.

I frowned at both her and the note. Gibson was only supposed to call me directly to avoid my underground lab being discovered. "Thank you."

"I'm sorry about your lunch being late the other day," Chelsea added. "I had a doctor's appointment for this cold. It's getting worse, but they can't do anything for me, so I came in to work, anyway. I know you don't like germs, so if you'd rather, I can go home."

Nothing would fix the girl yet. Either she'd beat it on her own or die, so I said, "Stay if you need the hours, otherwise you can go."

"Thanks, boss. I'll go home." Chelsea smiled weakly and closed the door, giving me privacy.

I dialed down to the lab immediately, and on the first ring, my call was answered. "Gibson, what's going on?"

"I've got the recipe Production needs to get Heromycin into vials. But we have a new problem, and we aren't talking about a contract any longer. This is a public health issue."

"I understand, doc. What's the problem?"

"Half the production staff is out sick. I need people, and I need them now."

"I'll get them to you. In the meantime, do what you can, and all of you geeks get double pay." Somehow.

Desperation and exhaustion tinged Gibson's voice. "It's not the money, Nick." He coughed and hung up.

Frustrated, I called human resources. Surely, my people manager could manage my people.

"Kelly here."

"It's Nick. I need you to open up jobs for Production. Don't put a limit on the openings, just get as many bodies as you can in here who know how to push buttons and drive a forklift."

"Sir, there isn't any funding available for the positions. They have to be approved by the department managers and worked into the budgets—"

"They're approved," I said, cutting her off. "Get them in here. I'll personally fund their payroll. Just do it."

"Yes, sir."

With Chuck Leach dead, I had no chance of securing a loan at Stars National Bank. At the time, I never considered if there were security cameras in Chuck's office, but since the police never contacted me, I figured they didn't know what I did, and since Chuck never touched a phone or computer to blacklist me during the incident, another bank should lend to me. But an incoming call from a wholesaler interrupted my planning.

"Mr. Barnes?"

"Yeah, I'm here. What can I do for you?"

"We're receiving record orders for Anycillin, but your sales department informs me that you still can't fulfill them. Do you have an estimated release date for us to tell the pharmacies?"

"Not yet. We're working diligently on it." Not that Anycillin would do any good against The Annihilator, but I wasn't compelled to relay that information.

"I heard about the new sickness tearing through your city. Such a shame. Shoot me an update when you have it."

"You'll find out as soon as we do. Don't worry." I ended the call and dialed an outside line.

Since I had a plan to secure funds, I was going scorched earth to save...this scorched earth. Chris, on leave from me or not, needed to help. I eagerly anticipated the excitement on my brother's face when I told him he could direct his television commercials—with a new small change. Instead of advertising antibiotics, he'd be urging people to apply for NBB's production floor. Chris's cell phone rang and rang with no answer. I dialed my sister-in-law's phone next.

"Nick?" Cyndi asked groggily.

"Hi, Cyndi. Just get off a shift?" Since her schedule was all over the place, I had no idea when she was coming or going from work.

Cyndi coughed. "I'm at the hospital with Chris. Didn't he tell you?"

"Tell me what?" I said slowly, brow furrowing.

"This morning, he moved into the intensive care unit. This sickness is scary. I hope someone finds out where it came from, and how to stop it soon. That's what you do, right, Nick? Make antibiotics to help people. Can you fix this?"

Okay, despite the world tipping over for everyone around me, hearing my sister-in-law beg for my help when all I'd ever heard from my family was insults felt...therapeutic. I basked in that for a moment. Then I puffed out my chest and gave her my best reassuring voice. "I'm working on it diligently as we speak. Don't worry about it. That's my job. Can you put Chris on the line, please?"

Gentle whimpers and a sniffle entered my ear.

"Cyndi?" I prompted.

She sobbed, wet sloppy heaves and sniffles. Uh, awkward.

"I need—" Another sob cut me off. "—Chris, please."

More sobs and a squeal. I waited until Cyndi composed herself. I checked my watch, grumbled at it still being melted as if it would someday fix itself, and a wet gasp and long exhale returned my attention to the phone.

"He's on a ventilator," Cyndi said.

The line went dead in my hand.

I cradled the handset and squeezed my fist. Flames engulfed my straining skin. Small potatoes I could handle. Medium potatoes were a bump in the road, but this went beyond large potatoes, and I just mashed them. Right here, right now. I pounded my desk with a flaming fist, again and again, but still, I didn't feel better. Important papers curled and ignited. Flames crawling along my desk opened my eyes wide. I vanquished the flames from my hand and patted out the sparks on the papers. I frowned at the singes.

If I couldn't advertise jobs fast enough, or hire people fast enough, then there was only one thing left for me to do. I had to slow down the demand. With a call down to public relations, I caught the manager, Jessica. "It's Nick. I need you to craft a campaign to slow down the demand for Anycillin. We don't have the staff to handle the sales right now." Any sales. I'd ordered production to stop.

Jessica scoffed. "You're worried about demand? I think you need to be more concerned about riots. Security is redirecting angry passersby and Housekeeping is helping fend off loiterers with mops and brooms. As this sickness progresses and Anycillin, their best shot, remains unavailable—this building will be ablaze soon."

Flame reignited my hand. What right did they have to destroy what I'd worked my whole life for? Who were they to judge my ability to do my job?

I didn't spray paint my server's house when she messed up my order. That'd be too much effort.

I didn't chainsaw my dry cleaner's sign when they failed to remove a stain. *Thanks, Lauren.*

I didn't drive over my barber's landscaping when the man trimmed my sides unevenly. I'd thought about it but settled on allowing him to fix the mistake.

I was only in business to help the public, those ungrateful... Well, if they wouldn't respect me, then I wouldn't respect them.

"Perhaps," Jessica continued, hesitantly, "it might be in our best interest to give the Anycillin formula to Novalite Pharmaceuticals to meet the demand, to ease the pressure on us. Just an idea."

"Novalite? Ted Bast—ion?" Oof, almost slipped on that one, Bastard. My turn to snort. No way would I give my most prized possession to that man. Jessica's suggestion made me want to burn her office down, even if she was only being helpful. "Never."

"Okay. How about negotiating with them to rent factory space and employees instead?"

If this were not a crisis, I'd almost consider promoting her. The woman had ideas—terrible ones, mostly—but good thinkers were hard to find. Nevertheless, her idea was pointless, since Anycillin wouldn't work against The Annihilator.

"I'll see what I can do. In the meantime, you get the public to calm down. That's your job."

"I know my job description." Jessica's voice sounded bitter, and she hung up on me.

If it weren't for the circumstances, I might've taken her out for a night or two. I liked that sauciness and spunk she had. Reminded me of the better part of Lauren. Now that I thought of it, I needed to give my ex a call.

22

Two Laurens

I RESTED IN MY penthouse, swirling a rum and Coke while watching my fish swim without a care in the world. A perfect slice of the ocean, a compatible mix of life with symbiotic relationships all over. As much as the corals and the invertebrates needed the fish, and the fish needed the corals and inverts, all of them knew who was boss.

I was the boss—of them, of this company, of this city. So why was I struggling to keep control? My parents hated me. My brother was sick by my own hand. My company was taking the heat for a product that wouldn't help. If I couldn't get Heromycin manufactured with any kind of speed, public health would be doomed and my future was shot. Out of the shit spiral my life had become, one thing might go right. I invited Lauren over for drinks, and she accepted.

Pooling all my frustration while waiting for her to arrive, I flicked a flame on my fingertip. Orange and red shimmied and danced while I gulped the last of my drink, ice cubes rattling in the glass when I set it down. With my other hand, I pinched the flames, and the orange glowed painlessly against my skin. How was I even seeing this? It made no sense. None of this demon-aura stuff made any sense.

A knock on the door was a welcome distraction. Snuffing the flame, I opened the door. Lauren's sweet smile lit up her painted face, and she'd chosen an outfit outlining her curves for miles—not all of them natural. But I missed every bit of her. I'd blame it on the drink later. For kicks, I used my demon vision to assess her, and sure enough, Lauren was human—a shade of thunderstorm gray. Was I surprised or relieved? The jury was still out.

"Hey, Nick, what did you want?" Lauren asked with a steamy gaze, bringing me right back to our happier times.

Honestly, I was surprised she'd agreed to come. After our last spat, I hadn't expected to hear a peep from her again. She twirled a dark brown lock on her slender finger. I wanted to grip that hair and yank back her head, giving me better access to her lips. Instead, I waved her inside.

Lauren entered while sliding her hands along my chest and up onto my shoulders. I closed my eyes, tipping my head back and picturing what I wanted to do next.

She whispered in my ear, "I missed you. Let's get a drink."

"You know what I like." I winked.

Lauren sashayed to my mini bar like old times, and I watched every shift and flicker under her tight dress. The fridge opened and closed. I returned to my leather armchair and lounged with an ankle resting on my knee, watching my fish. Slush shook in a cocktail shaker and filled a cup. Lauren served me a rum and Coke and made herself a strawberry daiquiri.

She lowered herself in the leather armchair next to me, and we sipped together in a comfortable but unusual silence. Anytime we had been in the same room together, we'd bickered—similar to how Mom and Dennis bickered, except Lauren wasn't a pushover and I wasn't an angry drunk. This distance had been good for us. Perspective. Priorities.

I swigged, the ice cubes clinking together.

"How's your drink?" she asked, slowly sipping.

"Strong as usual." Not strong enough. Her hot gaze followed me as I finished the last of my drink. Heat swirled behind my eyes, and I shifted my gaze before Lauren saw too much. Apparently, they weren't just red angries, they were red hornies, too.

"I've never admitted it, but your fish are pretty. You put a lot of thought into their habitat."

Guess I wasn't the only one who'd changed lately. "You never liked them before."

"I was too busy to admire them." She set her half-filled glass down on an end table and leaned toward me, showing her ample cleavage. "But I realize they're a part of you, like your identity. And if I'm to love you, I have to love them, too."

We were good together, a fun challenge, never boring. But where would that leave the two of us in the end? I still couldn't give her what she wanted. A bigger ring. More of my time. In fact, I think her engagement ring was still in the sand bed. I wasn't going to point that out.

But I still loved her.

Lauren's hand touched my thigh, and desire surged through my body. I jumped to my feet to escape her touch, hoping to calm the flooding fire before it was too late. The room tilted. Something was wrong. I swayed on unsteady legs. I'd had too much to drink, which baffled me. Lauren didn't mix them that strongly. Was this a side effect of becoming a demon? If Andras File didn't warn me that demons couldn't drink, I was going to…

"Vomit." I stumbled toward the bathroom, falling to my knees and crawling. I reached the sterile porcelain bowl—because anything less than sterile would make me vomit more—and I lifted the seat.

Heavy espadrilles on Lauren's feet thumped against the hardwood behind me. Resting my forehead against the bowl, I tilted my face to see her, but two Laurens appeared in my blurry double vision. Her arms crossed both her chests, and she stood, bearing weight on one foot of each Lauren. The smirk on her faces told me everything.

"Why?"

Staying in the doorway, one of the Laurens said, "I know why you called me, and it's never going to happen. I meant what I said—I never wanted to see your face again, but soon you'll see why I agreed to show up." Lauren walked away.

I vomited. My body tingled, and I checked myself for uncontrolled flames, but I found none. The room tilted on its axis and darkness dragged me down.

A MADDENING THROB IN my skull stirred my eyelids open. I blinked back the haze blurring my vision. That was beyond awful, and finding myself awake on the floor was so disgusting. Struggling to my knees, I used the toilet bowl to push myself to my feet, and I cringed at the wretched smell and flushed the toilet without looking. Although I wanted to incinerate my body from sleeping that close to vomit, I cleaned my mouth the old-fashioned way. In the mirror, I looked as exhausted as I felt, like I'd been hit by a truck. I hadn't had a bad drink like that in a while. I'd have to check the expiration date on the Coke. I checked my *melted* watch and groaned. With a headache, I shuffled to the living room while pressing a hand against the wall to support myself.

"Lauren?"

Nothing.

"Lauren, are you still here? What happened?"

A clock ticked in my kitchen. Lauren had arrived twelve hours ago. Funny, *all* I heard was the clock, even with my demon-enhanced hearing. Everything else was silent. Alarmed, I spun to my reef tank and gasped, seeing the reef shut down. The life-sustaining lights were off. Fishes' mouths gaped in panic at the surface from a lack of oxygen.

I rushed on wobbly legs to the equipment room. The power strips were unplugged. How the hell did that happen? Lunging, I plugged everything back in. Pumps hummed back to life. Lights flickered on. Water rushed through the PVC plumbing. I inspected the battery backup and found that had been unplugged also. I swiped my forearm against my sweating brow.

Checking for any more damage, my eyes settled on an empty bottle of vinegar sitting next to the sump. The gears in my head ground to a screeching halt. This was no accident. Equipment didn't unplug itself, but that could have been an accident. However, I was certain vinegar didn't uncap itself and pour itself deliberately into my sump.

Lauren.

That bitch. If anything survived the equipment failure, when I plugged it all back in, the vinegar would kill them all. I'd never underestimate her again.

I rushed to the outlet and unplugged the return pump. Panting, I lifted the back panel on the display tank to see the damage. From this angle, it didn't look good. With a terrified lump in my gut and an alarming wobble in my legs, I hurried to the living room and inspected the tank in the daylight. The corals were closed and quickly bleaching white. The fish floated sideways with a curve to their bodies and their mouths still. The crabs flipped upside down with their legs poking skyward like bones out of a graveyard.

They were all dead, even my treasured golden basslet.

My body engulfed with flames while tears watered my eyes. I dropped to my knees and unleashed a deafening demon-powered roar. With a terrifying thud and crackle, the glass blew. Over two thousand gallons of dead fish, coarse sand, and shards of glass gushed like a waterfall, flooding the hardwood floors throughout my condo. The glass wall to my condo cracked as well, allowing a cool autumn breeze to whistle.

Saltwater quickly drained out under the doors, likely causing untold structural damage to the floors below. My suit soaked up the water. Glass slivers bit into my legs, and blood trickled.

I wanted to call Chris, but my brother wouldn't care, even if he wasn't on a ventilator in the ICU. I considered calling my parents, but they wouldn't care either. And right now, I couldn't handle more Dennis-flavored insults.

Their little bodies were protected from my fire by the water, but it didn't matter. It was too late for them. My flames snuffed out, and my shoulders shook with sobs.

23

Transgression

Andras

RIPPLES OF NERVES DANCED in my gut. The king was a feisty guy on an average day, so I would rather be anywhere than here once the king learns the purpose of this visit. But the king wouldn't punish me...again. Not for this. I hoped. Just the thought of Glitter and all his rusty, gristle-and-char-covered tools made me shudder.

"Enter," The King of Hell ordered from the other side of his thick door.

With trembling hands, I ducked through the king's office door in Hell, displaying my natural iridescent purple dragon to conserve energy. The only thing about Nick Barnes I was jealous of—the new demon didn't have to glamour. And admittedly, the hair was swoon-worthy, too. The king was on the same wavelength about the effort involved, showing his natural red form.

"Sir, I have urgent news."

The king's curly tail swished as he filled a mug from the coffeepot. "Please tell me it's good news," the king pleaded with an airiness in his voice.

Too many negative things had been happening lately, and through no fault of my own, I was the demon in charge of angering the king.

"I'm afraid not. Nick Barnes killed a banker with a fire spear to the chest. The humans have surveillance footage showing the perpetrator and how the murder happened."

The king grumbled a few choice words. "It's been cleaned up?"

"Yes, sir."

"And that's the good news, am I right?" The king sipped his coffee.

The overhead lights dimmed and flickered before returning to normal operation. The king grimaced, glancing at the ceiling. "The electric grid is faulty. What's going on up there?"

"That's what I'm here to tell you. Our new aura demon, Nick Barnes—"

"Ah, yes, the first half-human to survive having his recessive demonic allele activated." The king interrupted, with a sparkle of interest, not unlike Nick's geeks. And now I realized I spent too much time with the newest demon. I'd picked up Nick's language.

"That's him. He created and released a bioweapon that's rapidly sickening the city."

The king's fluffy brows sunk. "What? How could this happen? You didn't stop him?" Flames erupted on the king's skin, turning him into a stereotypical demon, straight out of the fiction books. But those demons were child's play compared to the short one standing before me.

I chuckled nervously. "The demon I positioned in the lab failed to realize anything amiss was happening, since he's not a scientist, but when Nick took a trip to the lab and sifted through the microbiologist's paperwork, our demon heard Nick mumble the demons would be happy about his work."

The king's face burned a brighter red—as if that were possible—at the hateful stereotype. "Those goddamned angels spreading rumors... And they call us evil."

"I know. I agree entirely. But that's not the worst of it." After a quick pause to judge the king's state of mind—irritated beyond belief, I cautiously continued, "The bioweapon has begun killing its hosts. I'm afraid the balance of our world is being tipped toward the enemy."

The king gazed out the picture window at the darkened city with concern. His splayed palm trembled as he pressed it against the glass. No longer furious at Nick's insubordinate and grievous mistake, the king carried a solemn sadness on his features. "The angels far outnumber us. If they catch wind of this, it will be full war, with the humans caught in the middle. The humans frequently vocalize their fear of World War III. This would be a catastrophe far worse. A world-ender."

"An apocalypse."

"Precisely. Everything we know would be gone."

I had family down there in Hell City, too. Now everyone's safety was at risk. When the angels figured out what Nick had done.... I blocked those grizzly images from my mind. Some nightmares weren't worth visualizing until they materialized. "At your order, I'll do whatever is necessary to stop this, sir." Even if it broke my heart.

The king stepped up to me, craning his narrow neck. "Like humans, we cannot survive an apocalypse, as you call it. And such a grievous transgression must be answered for. But..." The king sighed and shook his head. "Our only aura demon is too valuable to terminate. He's our only hope. Understood?"

I nodded, relieved. "Clear as day, sir." I'd do anything the king ordered, but I didn't want to kill my best friend.

"Has he shown any memory regeneration from the spell?"

"None whatsoever. He has no idea of the evil lurking beneath his surface. I believe this transgression is merely coincidence."

The king grunted. "Excellent. In that case, the only reason he's roaming free on the surface is to fix this mess."

I saluted. "Your orders shall be carried out. Thank you, sir."

"Dismissed."

I left the office with a massive hurdle to scale. Somehow, I had to convince the stubborn Nick Barnes to change his plans, without telling him all the details of the war he'd inadvertently escalated. As he'd reminded me, I was no salesperson, but perhaps his window into our world would help him listen this time.

I wasn't entirely honest with the king. The fragile psyche of an arrogant, neurotic man carried a magical wall, holding back an apocalypse-craving alter ego. After these transgressions, I didn't believe in coincidence. I believed some of the spell's side effects were seeping through.

24

Break Me

Nick

When I was nine years old, just old enough to remember hiding behind closed doors and listening in on Chris's birds-and-the-bees talk with his buddies, I had spent an entire afternoon stacking a wicked house of cards. Each carefully placed at just the right angle to get them to stay. At the time, we didn't have the cat, so it was just me, a fuzzy understanding of gravity, and more time to kill than any mischievous boy ought to have.

Chris rushed through the house, yelling for Mom.

I shouted that she wasn't there and for Chris to stop running. I'd expected Chris to blunder right into my masterpiece on purpose. Instead, Big Brother stopped, smirked, and strolled up.

"Whatcha got there? Looks hard."

"It is. Go away."

"Why are you playing with stupid cards instead of your friends?" Before I could answer, Chris added, "Because you don't have any! Loser."

My lower lip quivered. "I'm telling Mom."

"Go ahead. Think she cares?"

"Get out of here!" I shouted, swallowing a sob. If I cried, Chris's teases would only get worse.

"Make me," Chris taunted.

I couldn't *make* my brother do anything. So, I did what any other nine-year-old with too much time on his hands would do. "If you stay, I'll tell Amber you were playing cards with me all weekend."

Chris backed up a step, genuine fear on his face. "You don't even know who she is. She's nothing to me. Go ahead, see if I care, you little brat." At the last second, Chris swung his arm near my fragile construction. The invisible enemy swooped in to destroy all I had built.

Many more times in my life, I'd lost everything, some more debilitating than others. I never suspected Lauren Hamil was capable of spiking my drink and masterminding a trick like that. But her message, as twisted and disgusting as it was, had been received loud and clear.

I couldn't leave my dead pets' bodies decomposing on the floor. They deserved better than that. I'd scooped up the remains and placed them gently in a plastic storage container until I decided what to do with them next. Then I'd stared at my sliced palms—the hands responsible for their deaths—and I swallowed back tears of agony.

I had texted my fish guy, telling him his services were no longer needed, and I tried not to break down in sobs when I explained they'd had an accident. Even though my fish guy would be the only person to empathize, I was not capable of owning up to what I'd done. Accident or not, tricked or not, I was a murderer.

Just like Chris had accused me of, even if that wasn't how he meant it.

While waiting for my fireproof vicuña suit to finish the wash cycle, I had opened an insurance claim for the damage to my condo, and after my clothes were back on my body, I'd called the building housekeeper. Normally, I'd never allow some random stranger to enter my private space and poke around, but this was too much for me to handle while on a serious time crunch. I had given her a phony excuse for the fire damage—faulty heater in the sump—and only shrugged at the cracked glass wall.

Andras entered my office. I never heard the knock, and I hadn't seen my demon friend since the gym, when he'd warned me the king was coming to recruit me into his services, which I politely declined and intended to do again.

"Sorry about your fish, Nick." Andras pulled out a chair across from my desk and settled his weight. A small gift box rested on his thigh.

"The irony is the amount of the insurance check would be enough to hire the staff I needed for R&D, as long as I skip the building repairs."

"Why do you need more geeks? I thought they have everything handled down there."

Since Andras would figure it out much sooner than later, I told him about the canceled government contract, the release of The Annihilator, and my failing plan for Heromycin, hoping for some insight to help. Not surprisingly, Andras didn't judge me—a perk of being a demon—so my Chief Information Officer was the only supporter I had left.

"But I won't have the check for a couple weeks," I added solemnly. "And Kelly said there's only been a handful of applicants. Too many people are too sick to bother applying. Even if I had the money now, the hiring and training process would take too long."

"But not getting the staff at all will slow down the recovery," Andras countered gently. "The best time to plant a tree was twenty years ago. The second best is now. You can't throw up your hands and walk away."

"Why not?" My will to fight finally broke. Except the tears in my eyes. I fought those pretty damned hard.

Andras leaned forward. "The King of Hell is very upset about all this. You can't mess with the natural order of death, especially something lacking strategy."

"Are you going to give me lines about God having a plan?"

My friend snorted. "The *king* does have a plan, and you're interfering. You have to fix this, or he will punish you, rather than work with you."

"Is this about the auras?"

"It's all connected." Andras stood and placed the small gift box on the desk in front of me. "Fix your mess and fix your hair. I need Nick Barnes on top of his game."

I raked a hand through my locks, confused and a little self-conscious. Despite Andras's deception, which I'd blamed on his terrible salesperson skills, he hadn't steered me wrong before. When the demon left, I opened the box and smiled, allowing those tears to fall, but now they weren't from anguish, they were gratitude. Then I chuckled, which turned into laughter, realizing a *demon*, of all things, lifted my spirits with a pep talk and gifted me a brand new watch to replace the melted one.

I dropped the old one in the trash and slipped on my new one. I could do this—a *demon* believed in me. I picked up the phone.

Chris's cell phone rang once and went to voicemail. Reluctantly, I tried Cyndi's cell. No answer either. I checked the time on my new watch and figured she was at work. Chris wouldn't still be in the hospital, would he? With a slow exhale and a firm grip on a pen, I dialed my parents.

"Nicky?" Mom answered with a quivering voice.

"Hello, Mom," I said, deadpan. They had, after all, disowned me.

"Wha...What are you calling here for?"

Apparently, they'd had the same sentiment—disowning meant no contact at all. If I planned to stop The Annihilator, both my parents and I needed to bury the ax for a few minutes.

"I need to speak with Chris, but I can't reach him."

"Oh, Nicky." Mom's voice was a waterfall of pain. After our blowout, I didn't think they cared so much. "You haven't heard."

Dennis's indecipherable grumbles penetrated my eardrum. I bet a Benjamin he was drunk again.

"Heard what?" I asked, standard defense-mode activated.

"Nick?" Dennis took the line from Mom, and I sucked in a breath, awaiting a torrent of insults, but I had my thick demon skin on, metaphorically speaking. "Chris told us what you did, you selfish asshole. Now he's dead. After I raised you, how could you murder my son? This is all your fault..."

The angry rant continued, but my brain blocked it out. The last I'd heard from Chris, my brother had been coughing just like the other victims of my bacteria and was placed on a ventilator in the intensive care unit.

I killed my own brother. Instead of saving the world, I was single-handedly destroying it.

"Nicky?" Mom said, having taken the phone back. "Did you hear? My baby is gone. You two never got along, so I want to hear your side. Did you release this plague?"

A debilitating force squeezed my chest. No longer trusting my voice, I squeaked out, "I have to go."

"Why, Nicky, why?" Mom pleaded. "We only wanted you to be normal."

I ended the call and inhaled deep breaths, counting backward from ten, but each one tore through my lungs like jagged glass. I stood on unsure feet, eyes glazed over.

My brother would never smile and ruffle my hair, or share an afternoon stacking cards or shooting hoops in the driveway. And now Chris would never make the commercial he'd been so excited about. He'd never have kids with the wife he loved. He'd never tell me he was proud of me.

Tears watered my vision, and I was drowning, sinking to the bottom of the ocean with anchors around my feet: Lauren, my parents, my fish, my company, and now the soft and gentle face of Chris. All of them pulling me down, helpless, where the water pressed against my chest, where my lungs burned for air, where the darkness snuffed out the light.

After all the malice and rejection I'd survived, why was the world playing a sick joke on me now? Did I have a paper sign on my back that said, 'Break me'?

Consider me officially snapped.

I'd show them.

All of them.

Fire erupted in my palms, and I gripped the edge of my desk and flipped it over, spraying paperwork, computer equipment, and pens all over the floor. I lifted my rolling chair and blindly launched it, punching holes in the drywall. I dragged my fiery hands along the wall, knocking down my degrees, awards, and photos of me with people who'd once impressed me. All meaningless. All worthless. All history.

With shallow breaths and hands burning, I surveyed the damage. My eye twitched at the misaligned mess on the floor and the defiant crooked photo still hanging on the wall.

The smoke detector overhead blared a warning, and I vanquished my fire. From the debris littering my office floor, I gripped a framed award. I relentlessly waved it at the obnoxious noise before the overhead system activated, ruining my suit again.

The noise ceased.

Tendrils of smoke lifted from the papers scattered on the floor. The chair smoldered in the wall.

There was only one place left for me to go.

25

It's Worse

I TELEPORTED THROUGH THE security measures of my underground lab and didn't bother gowning up. With my new plan, personal protective equipment no longer mattered, only hindered me from getting this done faster.

The inside of the lab smelled like its usual pleasant self—lemons and antiseptic—grounding me. The lights were bright, machines softly hummed, and across the room, a panel of lights blinked in an undefined pattern. The hazardous materials cabinet was closed, and from this distance, appeared to be locked.

The only geek in the room was Dr. Tyler Gibson in his marshmallow suit hunched over a microscope. Where was everyone else? Glimpsing the clear vault with the last test tube of bacteria, I had a second's regret at entering without my own gown, because I could die from the sickness just as easily as Chris had. Were all the geeks sick, too?

If my actions killed the entire specialized lab staff...

Pushing forward, my shiny shoes clattered against the tile floor, and Gibson's head whipped around in surprise.

"Hey, boss, I didn't hear the door open. Wait! You can't be in here without PPE!" The microbiologist stood and lifted his elbow to cover his cough, which, behind a mask and face shield, was entirely redundant.

I sent him a crooked smile. "I don't need it so long as you're wearing it."

Gibson didn't laugh. "Of course you do! It's not just each other we need protection from. If you get infected by these bacteria, at this concentration, it'll have catastrophic effects. And even if you didn't, by, I don't know, being inhuman, you're still risking the sterility of the lab. Please, Nick, return to the anteroom and gown up."

Time was of the essence, no more urgent than now. "Gibson, I need you to move."

"Please gown up. We've finished a series of tests on several batches of subjects, and the results were all the same."

Intrigued my lab manager hadn't noticed or learned the bacteria had already been released to the public, I asked, "What happened?"

"The bacteria spread like the wind. Airborne for sure, but it also spreads by bite."

I tilted my head. "Bite?"

"Like the droplets released with sneezes or coughs, bacteria are present in the saliva. After a batch of subjects was infected, several passed away within hours to days. Alarming, but not unusual. Somehow a percentage of those revived on their own, and that by itself is more concerning than relieving. We haven't singled out the mechanism of action yet."

"You told me about this already, but something else went wrong?" I couldn't imagine what. If my bacteria killed people, but some came back to life, certainly that would mean it wasn't *as bad* as it was meant to be. Like this was a partial failure, which turned out to be good news.

"This is the part that has kept me up at night, and frankly, has me baffled on how it works."

I didn't like hearing my genius microbiologist was baffled. Not at all.

"The subjects who died from the infection but reanimated appeared to retain their natural personality for a random period of time—anywhere from minutes to a couple of days."

"What happens after that?"

"They fall into a blind rage and bite others. The intent is to feed on raw flesh, and the bacteria absolutely spread through the bite."

The description sounded familiar, but I wasn't up to date on pop culture or comic books. "Are you saying zombies?"

The doctor gave me a double take as if I'd unlocked a new fear. "Well, uh, well, I don't think so. Zombies are walking dead, with only an active brain stem, seeking only to eat. They're slow, dumb, and predictable. Which are also, medically speaking, impossible."

Good to know.

"In our case, in reality here, the bite victim, if they escape being fed on, will repeat the pattern—an unpredictable length of illness gestation, where they can actively spread it through airborne particles. If they die, then they can reanimate. Those that do, within minutes to days, will convert from seemingly normal to the need to feed and spread the bacteria further. I think it's closer to rabies without the certain death."

"So...worse than zombies?"

"If we're comparing, yes. Absolutely more terrifying because of the unpredictability, and the fact that they can retain their natural selves until the urge to feed hits. Despite how horrifying this all sounds, I'm uncertain—optimistically doubtful—whether human subjects would reduce themselves to biting, but these mice—"

I pictured the critters as violent, greasy, feral creatures climbing into my bed... I shuttered and finished Gibson's sentence. "Are ticking time bombs."

"Precisely. Unless you know an infected person died, you won't know they were infected at all. The cough is only a symptom, and so common it can't truly be a marker. It might mean they'll be fine. It might not. I have this sinking feeling that if this gets out, no matter the government's intentions, it's going to cause everyone to ultimately catch it. The significantly dwindled population will be fighting to survive against the ones who turned...I can't believe I'm saying this...into zombies."

There was no way to be certain of our safety in public right now.

"Now you see why I'm concerned about you being here unprotected. Despite being the master of your universe, you can contract The Annihilator bacteria like everyone else. We need you, Nick, to facilitate a system of cure delivery for this bioweapon when the government gets it. Not just for the money—I don't care about that—but all those people..." Dr. Gibson's voice raised with a mounting panic. "So many potential deaths... How many people do you think will cuddle a lost loved one who miraculously returns from the dead? All of them. Every single person with a family is at risk of killing their own loved ones. So please, for my sake and yours, and for the safety of this whole damned planet, please put on a gown."

Without Gibson, I wouldn't be able to manufacture Heromycin. Next to my empathetic fish guy, who I'd reluctantly let go, and my supportive demon friend, Gibson was the third necessary person in my life, and the man was right. If the bacteria killed me, the world was doomed.

I chuckled. I was literally going to save the world. I'd be the hero I'd always wanted to be. "Sure thing."

Gibson smiled in relief and sat back down. I gowned up in the anteroom and headed straight for the acrylic vault. Like a responsible geek, it was locked. "Gibson? I need the key."

The microbiologist walked over with a frown. "Why this time?" He glanced in the vault and gasped. "The first test tube of bacteria is missing. You put it back, didn't you? Where is it?" Gibson bent at the waist and checked the floor as if I'd dropped it. "Hit the emergency evacuation button!" He pointed to the corner of the lab near the panel of blinking lights.

No one was around to respond.

I pulled at Gibson's shoulder to straighten him. "It's okay. I know where it is."

"You left this facility with it?" Gibson's voice was a few bars too high, and his eyes were bug wild. "Oh, no. Oh, no, no, this isn't happening. Oh, no, no, no."

"Haven't you checked the news lately?" I asked.

"I don't get out much." He gestured to a side door. "Been sleeping here most nights. The test tube is safe, right? You made sure to keep it safe?"

I unzipped my marshmallow suit and retrieved my cell phone, and I scrolled the local headlines about the sickness.

Gibson peered at the screen and read the titles with confusion. "The worst plague since the Black Death? The apocalypse is here? Nick...Is that why half the building is out sick? Oh, man. What did you do? This can't be true. This isn't happening. No, no, no." Gibson coughed like he was on the verge of an asthma attack. "I did this. I made this...this...this evil thing, and I shouldn't have. I knew better."

Gibson poked me in the chest with a gloved finger. "I should've destroyed it before someone like you managed to do this. Why I trusted you to do the right thing..." Gibson trailed off and jumped back as flames ignited all over my body, melting the white polyester suit off my fine luxury fibers.

"What the hell is going on?" Dr. Gibson placed a hand on his face shield, where his forehead would be. "I'm hallucinating. I'm coughing. The illness is free. My scientists and lab techs are sick. I have it. I have The Annihilator infection. I didn't know hallucination was a symptom. The mice couldn't say..." Gibson paced the tight space, glancing at me but keeping his distance. "I...I...can't be sick. I've been in here with filtered air. Something else...something in there"—he pointed accusingly at the locked hazardous materials cabinet—"Something in there fried my brain. I'm useless. My life is over. I need to find Anne!"

"Enough!" I threw a fireball in front of my employee. It landed in the stainless-steel sink and sizzled out. "Stop. Gibson, this is all real. I need you to head up the production of Heromycin. Cook that recipe and feed the people."

"Me? But I'm a researcher. This bacterium isn't studied in humans yet. If people are infected, I need you to bring me a few with consents signed, of course." Dr. Gibson's face was drawn as if he'd seen a ghost—or a demon.

"There's no time for research. There's only a cure."

"How...? How are you on fire?" A fresh fit of coughs overtook the geek, and he bent at the waist until he recovered.

The smoke alarms activated from my flames, and within seconds, white dust sprayed down from the ceiling. Alarms rang and strobe lights flashed.

The geek held a hand over his head to protect his hairnet from the dust. Not sure why. He shouted, "We have to get out of here!"

"No." The work wasn't done yet. No throwing in the towel—not after how far I'd gotten, how much I'd sacrificed. The world depended on me, and I depended on Gibson. "I'll get the cleanup guy to take care of this, and you'll get back to work. Now, give me the keys."

Dr. Gibson's wild eyes locked on me. "You can flame-on like Johnny Storm. You infected the public with deadly experimental bacteria that kills and reanimates mice, and you want to walk away with the *second* vial?"

I stepped forward and dusted off my shoulders to keep the intimidating flame roiling. "I came for Heromycin."

"Why? Since I rushed the write up for Production, I haven't finished creating the redundant sample yet. There's only enough to cure one person, and from what you showed me, thousands are infected already." Gibson coughed again, and I was surprised the extinguishing agent wasn't bothering my lungs.

I didn't have time to focus my best worker. Every moment I spent calming Gibson was another moment delaying the production. "I don't have to justify anything to you."

Dr. Gibson scoffed. Out of derision or dust, I wasn't sure. "You know what? I quit. I will no longer be part of something so damned evil that Hell itself must've spat it back out. Look at you! You're on fire but not screaming in pain or dying! What are you?"

I didn't have time to ease him into my hidden world, and there was no going back from this. "You can't quit on me. We have work to do. Don't lose sight of the bigger plan here. Give me the keys."

Gibson approached until my heat steamed his visor. "Turn off your flame and let me out."

"No." My flame grew just to spite him.

Gibson backed up a step. "Don't make me do something I'll regret."

"Like what?" The strobe lights were giving me a headache. And I didn't react to threats well. I tried. I truly did.

THE MICROBIOLOGIST RETREATED FROM my burning body and picked up a stool, holding it like a weapon, while the white powder continued to blast us from above. His panicked breaths steamed his visor. "Let me out or I'm calling the police!"

No matter how many terrible things I had done, whether I admitted them or carried guilt over them, I drew the line at allowing the public to castrate me for this. The CDC counted on me to fix the problem. That was the only reason I wasn't in prison now. Andras and The King counted on me to fix this, or an unspecified punishment awaited me. After I saw that glittery and unicorn-colored hair guy with a barbecue skewer, I figured three-hots-and-a-cot was the better option.

If Gibson rejected me... If my Gibson failed *me*? Then I couldn't fix this at all, and my favorite geek would destroy me with this information. No longer the hero, I'd be the villain—and Dennis would've been right in predicting my future. *It means you're a failure, you ungrateful, stubborn bastard.*

Failure.

Furious at Gibson's threat of betrayal, anger accumulated like a festering boil on the surface of my skin—metaphorically, not literally, because that would be gross enough to make me vomit, and once a decade was enough. The accumulated pressure exploded flames out from my body, sending a shock wave through the whole lab, same as the one that sent Heather Brush through a stone wall.

Glass shattered, cabinets buckled, and the microbiologist flew backward. But still the white powder sprayed.

After giving the geek a reality check, I stepped over his subdued body and approached the vault. It hadn't been designed to be blast-proof. I plucked away shards of cracked acrylic and lifted out the intact test tube of Heromycin.

Dr. Gibson had been coughing, and I believed he had the contagious bacterial infection. With confirmation the sickness spread through droplets in the air, I was infected, too. At any moment, the coughs would seize me, and in my hand was the only cure.

Gibson had spread himself too thin preparing the recipe for Production, studying the mice, and managing the ill workers. He never finished crafting the redundant antibiotic.

If I chugged this down myself, I'd continue the depressing battle to find production workers to fulfill the orders as Dr. Gibson supplied. Or I could hand it over to Ted Bastard's Novalite Pharmaceuticals to mass produce for the public. But then Ted Bastard would get the accolades for saving the world.

I had been willing to let Chris take the glory, figuring most people would know I was behind it all, anyway. But since I lost my girlfriend, both my parents, my prized fish, my brother, and my best geek's loyalty, could I really hand the glory to Ted?

I swirled the vial in my hand.

When I was in my late teens, I'd already begun my second entrepreneurial adventure. The first one, mowing lawns, was too competitive and too much hard labor—not how I wanted to spend my time, although trimming hedges into orderly lines was cathartic.

"You're doing what this time?" Chris asked with an attitude of superiority.

I had just gotten home with a brand-new turntable, driven in my beat-up car that I'd saved for, and I set up in the garage on a pair of sawhorses. Resting on the turntable was my favorite childhood toy, a Magic 8-Ball. I'd consulted the wisdom of the triangle before setting up in the garage, asking if my new venture was at risk of demolition by any family members. The 8-Ball had told me 'Ask again later' three times before settling on 'My sources say no.' So, I set up to practice far from Dennis's sensitive ears.

"I'm going to DJ events," I told Chris.

"Huh," Chris said. For the first time, he didn't tease me. "And how'd you get this turntable?" He leaned, inspecting the new unit. With a wide grin, Chris tapped the crossfader and slid an invisible disc, pretending to crab scratch.

"I worked for it," I said dryly.

Chris bobbed his head to a melody only he could hear and shouted, "Dad!"

Dennis climbed down the garage stairs connected to the kitchen, grumbling and holding a cup of coffee. Now knowing Dennis, I figured that cup was spiked with liquor. It was early on a Saturday morning. Too early to be bothering Dennis.

I reluctantly allowed my brother to continue playing. The sooner he bored himself of my new toy, the sooner I could get to work.

"What is it this time?" Dennis sipped from his coffee, wearing a ragged T-shirt, torn jeans, and scruffy slippers. The weekend was his chance to dress like...well, like a plumber with different footwear.

"I want to join Nick's business."

Dennis popped a brow. "Is that so? What are you up to now, Nick?"

"I'm going to DJ parties. It's not a two-person job."

"Nonsense," Dennis said. "All businesses need to grow to succeed. My boss has four plumbers on staff. Four. We're so busy that without us, he'd have quit from the stress." I had been still in high school with limited business experience at the time, but I was certain that was not how it worked even then. "Chris only wants to do you a favor."

"But—" I protested.

"You should thank him." Dennis cut me off. "And a good brother sees that and understands, while graciously accepting the help."

I sighed. Chris wasn't the business owner type, but if he really wanted to help me grow and succeed, who was I to deny him that? "Fine. Fifty-fifty split on the profits after my initial costs are recouped."

"Whatever." Chris spun discs that weren't there, and with a harsh and completely unnecessary flip of some switches, the turntable fell over, sending my 8-Ball flying and landing with a crack. Liquid leaked out of the sad

8-Ball like a dying friend, a friend whose advice led to its own death.

The turntable crashed onto the concrete floor. Instinctually, I rushed to pick it up, coddling it like an injured pet, but the corner was smashed. Hopeful the damage was cosmetic, I turned it on, but it was silent. I tested the switches, and nothing.

After a second's silent shock, Chris broke out laughing.

"Dad!" I whined, tears filling my lids.

Dennis sipped from his coffee, disinterestedly observing the damage. After a swallow, Dennis said, "I guess that'll teach you to be careful of who you choose to do business with."

"He needs to pay for the damage!" I demanded. "And he killed my 8-Ball!"

Chris only smirked.

"And this is a lesson in humility. Flaunting your success only leads to failure. You're two for two so far. Clean up that mess." Dennis retreated to the kitchen.

I frowned. I didn't fail at the lawn mowing company. I'd simply moved on. The loss of my DJ business before it started wasn't my fault.

Alone with my brother, Chris laughed and laughed. "Always a loser."

My hand formed a fist, and I stared at it.

Forced to give up half my business, only to lose it all in the blink of an eye. Chris needed to pay somehow. I launched at my brother and pounded him. We fell to the floor and rolled in the skirmish. Debris collected in my hair and clung to my clothes. Blood pooled at my knuckles, and Chris could only try to parry the blows with his face turning beat red. No longer laughing, my big brother desperately tried to stop the onslaught, but I couldn't quit until I unleashed all the years of torment.

Chris slumped, defeated. And I slowed my assault. His features were puffy and a funny shade of red. His lip split, and his eye swelled shut.

Panting, I stood. "Maybe now you'll think twice about destroying my stuff."

Chris's words were wet from blood and snot. "You're just a stupid asshole. Dad's right about you."

The last thing Chris had said to me before he died was, I'll go down in history as the world's greatest mass murderer. Words like those were hard to forget.

The test tube in my hand glistened red under the fluorescent lights. I swirled the liquid. Sharing my successes with people who didn't deserve them had done nothing but cause me great loss—friendships, family, relationships, pets—and after all I had given up, I learned one thing from Dennis. I wasn't going to do any business with the competition, Ted Bastard.

My future was in my own hands, and I couldn't fix anything if I were dead, in prison, or spending time with that glittery dude in Hell.

I uncorked the test tube and drank it all. Tossing the empty against the wall, it shattered and fell silently onto a cushioning pile of powder.

Gibson's body hadn't moved and seeing my friend lying there like my old leaking Magic 8-Ball speared me in the gut. I could've done so much more, tried harder to explain. I bent down next to my friend and removed the protective face shield. Despite myself, I checked for a pulse at his throat, but I couldn't find one.

My knees gave out, and I dropped to the floor. What had I done? What was I going to tell Gibson's wife?

26
Controlled

Andras

IN THE NORTH WING of Hell, the current location of torture due to ongoing remodeling in the south wing, I pounded a fist against a dungeon door, interrupting screams of agony. When the king summoned, I answered, no matter how unpleasant or awkward the location. With how perilous the surface had become, my inner essence, a similar construct to a human's soul, feared the king's wrath.

The screams stopped, and the king boomed, "Enter."

I pushed back the squeaking old oak door and stepped inside, careful to avoid the blood spray and spittle. Glitter was bright and playful on the outside, but the unusual responses I always received from him unsettled me. With the king at least you knew where you stood. With Glitter—he'd do anything as ordered and not bat a sparkly eyelash.

The king, currently displaying his human glamour, stepped away from inspecting the torturemaster's work and nodded for Glitter to resume. But thankfully, Glitter waited until the king and I moved into the hallway. The screams were drowned out by the door closing.

"Nick Barnes," the king started and finished as if that was all that needed to be said.

My essence flattened to my feet. If it could, it would've liquefied out through my toes and through the floor below us. The scalding saunas down there sounded more pleasant than where this conversation was headed.

"He doesn't act like his father, a great obedient soldier true to the cause. Are you certain, after all that has come to pass and his alarming side effects, that this young man is his son?"

I had been certain until the king questioned my judgment. I cleared my throat. "Yes, sir."

"Nick made a mess up there. Souls are releasing from their vessels at speeds I haven't seen for centuries. Under different circumstances, I'd relish the effortless gain to our side, but the souls are going the wrong way." The king growled his frustration.

"What are your orders, sir?"

"Regroup the contract demons to focus on the easiest targets first. We need numbers, and I want Heather back on the field. Pull who you can spare from the Field Agents. Get the teams ready to deploy on the hunt to destroy those reanimated creatures and slow this infection. Arm them with topside weapons. Bullets are easier to explain than piles of burned corpses lying around, at least in these modern times."

"Yes, sir. I shall issue the commands at once." I turned to leave, but the king's next question stilled my steps.

"Is Nick ready to join the ranks and clean up his own mess?"

A chill rippled down my spine. Disappointing the king was a game of Russian roulette, except five of the six chambers contained a round. Management always got the blame, and I didn't want to be Glitter's next plaything. "He is not, sir."

"Not ready?" the king repeated, astonished. "The son of the greatest aura demon in history is not ready? I understand such strength is a rush for a human, but now I own him, and he will obey. Bring him to me by all means necessary."

"Copy that."

Before I moved an inch, the king said, "Oh, Andras?"

"Yes, sir?"

"If he's still uncooperative, send him to have his memory wiped."

I didn't like the idea of having my friend's memory erased. What if Nick forgot about me, too? I considered Nick an actual friend, not just an assignment. There weren't enough friends down here. Damned demons.

"And if the memory wipe is necessary," the king continued, "I task you with creating new memories in place of the dangerous ones. You know him better than all of us. I trust you can assemble something that will work for him?"

I smiled as if I'd been given a fresh muskrat burger straight off the grill. Normally, the memory demons performed the delicate procedure. Only by dumb luck was I allowed to do it, and I'd fix my friend's future without erasing me. Perfect. "Can I have a little fun with him?"

The King of Hell's lips pulled wide. "Planning on locking him in a room full of mice?"

Tempting. "Not exactly."

"Make sure the erase is permanent. Permission is granted to have whatever fun you choose. What else is Hell for?"

I spun on my heel and teleported away at once, because keeping the king waiting was never wise. Knowing Nick would never surrender voluntarily, I already knew which memories to erase and what new ones I'd implant. Nick was in desperate need of an ego chop.

27

The Truth

Nick

THE FLAME RETARDANTS PETERED down to a drizzle, and sprinkles fell to the floor like gentle snowflakes. My finger swiped at the powder, seeking the cold of snow, but no feeling penetrated my skin. An emptiness, a nothing. I could've swiped dust or sand and noticed no difference.

Any minute now, Dr. Gibson would wake up. The microbiologist wasn't dead. He couldn't be. The man just absorbed a strong shock to the system and suffered head trauma. Just a bump to the old noggin. He only needed a few more moments to wake himself. Then everything would be fine. Completely fine. Back to the way things used to be.

"Nick." Andras's voice lifted my heavy head.

"How did you get in here?" I asked absently, knowing only a few staff knew about the location and even fewer had access through the handprint scanner.

"There's a massive hole in the wall. I walked over debris."

Where the front door had been was blown to bits. Huh.

"If I wanted to, I could've teleported inside." Andras leaned down on his haunches next to me and rested a heavy hand on my shoulder.

"How did you know this place existed?" I had been so careful with that information. Who leaked it?

"We've been watching you for a while. What are we looking at here?"

"The white flakes falling like snow, covering everything, erasing all I've done." The final sprinkles of dust fell after the fire suppression system had discharged.

"Alright, Nick. Time to get up and join the ranks." Meaty hands lifted me to my feet. "We need to make a plan now. Your time is up."

"Time? What time? Can't you see what I've done?" I turned my head toward Gibson's prone form. "It's too late to do anything now."

Andras sighed. "The sickness is spreading. People are dying. I need you to come up with a solution, any solution, to stop this in its tracks."

"Hero—mycin!" I sang the name like a wrestling announcer.

"Great. That's a start. Where are you on getting it to the public?"

I weakly gestured to the lab counter where Dr. Gibson left his paperwork. "That's all there is. Numbers and letters on those papers. A recipe and an empty production facility. No materials. No money for materials. No materials available if I had money."

Andras sighed. "Then we're done here. This...situation no longer concerns you. We must go."

"What doesn't concern me? My building? My home? My family? My fish?"

"All the above."

I wasn't going to be dragged to Hell. Not yet. I had booze to drink and…and…something. Whatever the punishment was, I didn't want it, and Andras couldn't force me to do anything or go anywhere. Especially not that short stocky dude they called a king. How could that king instill enough fear to control demons?

"My orders are to bring you in by all means necessary. If you won't come willingly, this will not be pleasant for you."

I chuckled. "Are you threatening me now? That's rich."

Andras reached out a supportive hand, but I refused it with a furrow on my brow.

"Orders are orders. This isn't personal."

"It's never been personal," I said sharply. "From the moment you met me, I was your order, or mission, or whatever."

"Assignment."

That didn't help any. "What kind of friend are you if you've been secretly spying on me for that puny king? That's all I've ever been to you, an assignment."

"That's not true, which is why we're having this discussion, and I haven't already subdued you."

"Subdued? Am I a wild gorilla? Tell me how you really feel. Tell me what you really think of me. I'm an animal. A monster. I'm every bit the demon you turned me into—this curse! You cursed me! And I'm not going to be your prisoner or The King of Hell's new toy. As the lovely Brits like to say, piss off!" Flames ignited on my fist.

"The spell you were subjected to did not make you a demon."

The flames reduced. "What?"

"Demon Spell 79,513 didn't convert you. It activated your dormant genetic code, awakening your demon abilities—namely, reading auras. The small benefits I told you about—wielding fire and teleporting—weren't a bargaining chip. You were always half demon. And now, like your father before you, The King of Hell needs you in his ranks."

I snorted. "Dennis has his bad days, but the last thing I'd call him is a demon. No, he loves his Good Book too much for that, and he's not crafty enough to have kept a secret for all these years."

"Not Dennis."

I shook my head in utter disbelief. "Dennis Barnes isn't my father. Is that what you're telling me?" The flames flickered out entirely.

"Precisely."

"Is Stella my mother? Chris my brother? Or is that whole family thing bullshit, too?" I didn't want to admit it, but if Dennis wasn't my father, my childhood made much more sense.

"Yes, they are."

I exhaled a deep breath. "I can't believe any of this."

"Then they can tell you themselves. Come here and hold my hand tight." Andras held out a palm expectantly.

Following the politeness of an offered hand and suddenly feeling unstable on my feet, I grabbed the demon's hand. Andras held tight.

"What are you—" The familiar shudder whisked me away from the lab and dropped us onto the front lawn of my parents' house in the suburbs. It was early evening with a cold autumn breeze, but the chill no longer bothered me.

But this location did. With horror, I said, "What the hell are we doing here?"

"Go knock."

"You want me to knock on that door and say 'Hey, Mom. So you cheated on Dennis, and I'm the son of a demon? Cool, good times.'?"

"Not how I would word it, but sure."

I shook my head, ready to teleport my own ass back to my lab, when the front door opened.

Mom stood on the porch, wearing a long nightgown, arms folded over her chest, bracing against the cold air. Her face was closed off, dead. "Nick, what are you doing here?"

Dennis pushed his way through the door and jutted a fat finger at me. "You're not welcome here, you bastard."

"Is it true?" I asked, ignoring the inflammatory moniker I'd heard for decades.

"Is what true?" Mom asked, exchanging a glance with the towering Andras next to me. She sounded empty inside, as if Chris's death had hollowed her out. There was nothing left for me in her heart.

Anger sizzled under my skin. They never cared about me at all. I swirled the heat behind my eyes to show them exactly why I was here.

Mom gasped.

Dennis shook his head. "Figures. What a waste. See honey, all those years for nothing. I told you this would happen."

"You knew about this?" I asked, approaching the door. All those times Dennis called me that slur now seemed so blatantly obvious. "All this time, you knew you weren't my father, but you chose to keep that from me. Why?"

Dennis glanced up at Andras. "We had our orders."

"Wait!" I pinched the bridge of my nose. "You were in on this? All of you knew about this?" The disbelief, the betrayal was overwhelming, but one question above all haunted me. "Mom, if I were Dennis's son, would you have treated me better, or was Chris always destined to be the golden child?"

Mom gasped again. "Don't you speak ill of the dead. It's bad luck. And his death is your fault, you..., you..."

"Go ahead, Mom. Say it."

Not that I hadn't heard the word my whole damned life.

"Monster," she spat out.

That wasn't what I expected, but after the day I'd had, I wasn't above playing dirty. "Cheater."

At the side of the house, Odie the elephant appeared again. Just great. Another judgmental face here to gloat. Useless, overactive, waste of an imagination.

"That's enough," Dennis interrupted. "You get off my property and never return!"

"I'm surprised you," I said back to the drunk, "You, of all people, forgave her sin."

The man approached, fists clenched, and I caught a whiff of the bottled brew on his breath. Generally I wouldn't get this close, but I had extra strength in my pocket these days.

"Are you up to six...seven drinks? Or are you knocking back more these days?" I taunted.

"Shut your mouth." Dennis swung hard with a right hook. His drunken movements were slow, even for a human, and I easily dodged.

While keeping an eye on Dennis's embarrassing movements, I watched Odie shuffle out of the bent bushes and approach Andras. What the hell kind of imaginary...?

With a blurring shudder, Odysseus shifted into a human. No longer enormous or gray, Odie was bald, thin, and wore jeans and a T-shirt—a regular, ordinary human, one I'd never look at twice if it weren't for what he looked like a minute ago. I froze, stock-still, and in my utter stupor, Dennis clocked me in the eye.

"God damn it. Ow." I covered my injury with my hand and bent briefly at the waist.

Dennis lost his balance after the strike. He climbed back to his unsteady feet, fist raised to strike again. This time, when Dennis lunged, I grabbed the man's fist and shoved him to the ground. Something way more important had just happened.

I approached Andras and my invisible childhood friend. I cleared my throat. "Uh, Andras?"

Both Andras and Odie turned to me. This was so far beyond creepy.

I whispered, hooking a thumb at the once-elephant. "Can you see him?"

"Of course I can. He's a shifter. One of a handful who can remain invisible when they choose, which is why he was assigned to be the guardian."

I shook my head and stared at my new imaginary friend. "You're real? All this time I didn't imagine you?"

Odie smiled that obnoxious smirk. Yep. It was him alright.

"Can you talk?" I turned to Andras. "Does he talk?"

"I can speak. I find no reason to," Odie said.

My lips parted.

"Wha—?" Dennis yelled. "What are you doing here? Get off my lawn!" He scurried on the ground like an inebriated fool.

"Honey, get in here now!" Mom shouted.

The people who raised me—poorly, I might add—rushed inside the family home and slammed the door. I figured I'd never be allowed back again, especially after flashing my demon eyes at them. At this point, I had more pressing issues to address. Like that guardian label.

"If you were assigned to protect me, then why didn't you ever help? You saw what Dennis did to me all those years! You watched what Chris did! And Mom always turned a blind eye. Tell me why you didn't help."

"I was assigned to protect them from you, because your father didn't know if you possessed the dormant demon gene."

Ouch. "I was a kid."

"Your father sent me to you. He told me you'd need answers, and on that front, your mom didn't cheat. Your parents were on a break when she met your father. Dennis and Stella agreed to raise you as their own, little brother to Chris, in hopes they could be positive role models in your life and minimize the demon influence in you."

My head swam. "What happened to my real father?"

"The opposition caught Ronove during a covert assignment and murdered him."

"You're certain?" To be told one moment my father wasn't my father and the next that my real father was dead gave me whiplash.

"Biologically they can't lie, so we are certain."

This was just too much. My whole life was a lie. Nothing was as it seemed, but weirdly, many things made so much more sense. Despite being half-brothers, Chris treated me like a neighborhood pest. Dennis decided long ago I was a burden, rather than his child. Mom always pushed me to do what she wanted, and now I knew why: she was terrified I'd become a demon, like my real father.

I raked a hand through my sticky locks, and with a grimace, brushed white powder off my hands and shoulders. My suit was a mess. I patted and smacked at the fabric in desperation to clean myself. The fire suppression powder was horrifyingly messy. I gasped. "Gibson! We left Gibson at the lab. I have to go back."

Without another second wasted on my messed-up life, I teleported back to where I'd left my best geek.

28

It's Here

I CLIMBED OVER THE rubble that used to be my anteroom. Sparks dripped from the swinging light fixtures. White powder coated every surface like a blanket of fresh snow. All the equipment was destroyed, but I only cared about one thing at the moment.

The crunching of shoes behind me turned my head. Andras had followed, but not Odie, the damned invisible elephant in the room who turned out to be a real elephant—a shifter. Demons and angels were hard enough to wrap my brain around, but shifters? I'd unpack that another time.

A cough came from the floor.

"Gibson?" I rushed over and squatted down next to my geek's head. "You okay?"

Gibson's eyes fluttered open, and he coughed again, dragging in a raspy breath. "Nick?"

I glanced at the demon over my shoulder, eyes wide, as if Andras had somehow fixed him just when I needed that win, and I was beyond relieved. Andras only shrugged. I helped Gibson to his feet. He wobbled on unsteady feet and lowered himself onto a stool.

I brushed his shoulders clear. The shield was pointless now, so I tore it off and helped him straighten his glasses.

I removed his mask so he could breathe better. "I'm so glad you're okay. For a minute there, I thought I'd...never mind."

Gibson's wild eyes scanned the demolished lab. A sparking light fixture fell to the floor with a metallic crash. Another light flickered, and smoldering patches lit the mangled lab like an eerie cave, suffocatingly small and too dark for comfort. "What happened?"

Clearly, he didn't remember our fight or the fact that he'd quit his job. I might've hit him a little too hard, but I used that to my advantage. "You're going to save the world with Heromycin. Ready to join the winning team?"

Dr. Gibson leaned on the stool as if his balance was off kilter, and he steadied himself against the counter. "What happened to the lab?"

"Accidents happen. I can have it rebuilt over the weekend if you're with me. Can I count on you?"

Gibson swayed. "Under one condition."

"Name it."

"You stop..." Gibson shifted. He hadn't regained himself after that knock to the old noggin, but considering the circumstances, I was patient. I would be infinitely patient with this man, considering I'd thought I lost him. "Stop everything. We work on antibiotics only. That's what I signed up for." His words were breathy, as if speaking was work. After getting his bell rung, I expected that.

"Done." And I meant it. I had cash coming soon from the insurance settlement. I had demand for Heromycin, and I had the winning formula.

"What happened to...my lab? It's about to collapse—smolderin' an' smokin'. Did you...?" The dangling light fixture sparked and crumbled plaster thumped to the floor. A smoky haze filled the room.

"Gibson, let's get out of here. Grab the recipe and any documents that haven't been destroyed."

"That's not possible," Andras stood firm with a frown.

I faced my friend. "Isn't this what you wanted—for me to fix my mess? Well, I am. We are. Now move."

"I have orders to terminate any reanimated on sight. He cannot leave this room."

"Reanimated?" Gibson leaned again, and he cocked his head. "Are you talking about..my mice? What's wrong with...mice? Hey... you can't...be in here without your personal...protective...equip..."

"Come with me, Nick," Andras said, holding out a hand, as if urging a child away from a dangerous animal.

"That's a negative, big guy. I have a company to repair and a drug to mass produce."

Having finally un-rung his bell, Gibson stood. It was great to see him up and at 'em again. I made a placating gesture toward Gibson to take it easy. "It's okay. I'm going to fix it. I'm going to fix everything."

"Nick," Andras's tone was a warning. "Get back."

Gibson flipped his head side to side as if cracking his neck or loosening muscles. When he finished, he opened his eyes, but I couldn't recognize him. Something was very wrong with the geek. An awful, throaty gargle came from his open mouth.

"Gibson?"

My geek didn't respond. His eyes were vacant, his skin translucent. And he did nothing but make that throaty noise.

"Gibson, can you hear me?"

My friend shuffled toward me, arms raised out to me, but I hesitated to help him return to his seat. Just before he reached me, Andras shoved me away, and a spark of light glinted against a blade in Andras's hand.

"What's going on? Stop, both of you!" I grabbed at the bigger man's thick biceps before he could strike, but my efforts were like tossing a yarn lasso at a bull. With no effort at all, Andras flicked his wrist, and a red line formed across Dr. Gibson's throat.

"What are you doing? I need him!" I shouted in horror.

Gibson didn't react to the wound. His throaty gargle only became stifled. His arms dropped to his sides. The front of his marshmallow suit washed red, and after another shuffle of unsteady feet, Gibson's head fell off his shoulders. His body tipped over into a cloud of powder.

With a surge of fury, no longer capable of being contained, flames ignited over my hands.

Andras cleaned his blade on a piece of debris and secured it at his waist, seemingly unconcerned with my threat. He explained, "Gibson reanimated, and orders are to destroy on sight. No one is immune, no matter how important."

"You're saying he died and came back? He didn't die. I never saw his white aura..." I trailed off, seeing piles of white powder covering everything and realizing the spray of flame retardant would've obstructed my view of the aura gently floating away. I also hadn't found a pulse at his throat, but I wasn't a doctor.

I'd killed Dr. Tyler Gibson.

The remaining blood trickled off the microbiologist's severed neck and dripped to the floor.

"Reanimated are what humans erroneously call zombies; zombies come back from the dead to feed and spread their virus. Reanimated return from the dead and may or may not convert into a mindless cannibal intent on spreading their virus. See the difference?"

Not really, no. "How do you know so much about this?"

"Look, I don't have time to give you a rundown of the world around you. Let's just say, for brevity, this isn't the first zombie apocalypse."

"You just said they're not—"

"It's time to go. The king requires your cooperation now."

I took a step back, shaking my head. "I can't trust you. You lied to me when I hired you, and you lied about what you were doing in my building. You refrained from telling me you're a damned demon and that there's a Hell portal in my broom closet. You declined to reveal you knew about my secret lab. You tell me my dad isn't my dad, and now you killed my best geek. For the last time, I've heard enough. Get out of my lab!"

Andras approached, and I was done warning him. I formed a fireball in each hand and unleashed them straight at Andras, knocking him back off his feet. The big demon crashed against the hazardous materials cabinet, buckling the door, and he flinched as he regained his footing.

I smirked. "I warned you."

Andras unbuttoned his suit coat. "If this is what I must do, then so be it."

The last thing I wanted was Andras dead, too, but I couldn't contain the fury and betrayal and...hopelessness. "I'm not holding back, my friend."

"Please don't." Andras smirked in challenge.

I flung two more fireballs at Andras, but this time, the demon had braced himself. The flaming orbs bounced off his chest, fell to the damaged floor, and sizzled out with the flame-retardant powder, reminding me of attacking a black bear with a squirt gun. Disbelief pulled my features. If that didn't just kick the socks off my ego, I didn't know what else could.

Andras hurled a single fireball at me, and all I had time to do was cover my face with my forearms to stop myself from being thrown backward. Newsflash: it didn't work. My body launched through the air and slammed into the clear vault, knocking the last test tube of The Annihilator free.

I fell to the floor, and the corked glass went with me, shattering on impact. Liquid from the broken tube splashed next to my knee.

It was gone.

The last chance to easily convert the sample to a new bacterium for the government was over, and now I was going to become a zombie, so my flames engulfed my body in a blindingly bright orange and white ball of protective fire. Anger helped sterilize me. And no one gave me orders and destroyed everything I stood for without payment. With a snarl on my lips, I threw the massive wall of fire at the demon.

Andras, standing firm against the onslaught, had the gall to check his watch while my fire pummeled his chest.

Fury surged, and I mustered up every last ounce of power I had and struck the demon again. Andras held out a hand as if shielding the sun from his eyes. The level of failure my efforts had was crushing. After draining all my strength for the fire, I couldn't manifest another fireball.

"I'm here to enforce the deal we made, but now the chance to volunteer is over."

My limbs were restricted. I could wriggle, but invisible binds held my ankles, wrists, and forearms. Even with everything I'd just experienced, I fought against the mystic ties. "What's going on? What did you do to me?"

Andras closed the distance between us, eyes locked on me and not bothering to watch his footing. With a twist of his hand, the binds tightened, and pain flourished at the pressure points.

"If you're concerned with inconveniencing me further, remember the pocket-sized King of Hell?" I nodded, unable to speak through the pain. "I am the kitten to the King of Hell's hawk. The fish to the grizzly bear. The krill to the blue whale. Understand now?"

I nodded again, and the pain eased as the invisible binds holding me lessened. "I understand you plan to eat me."

With a sigh, Andras said, "Time's up to fix your mess. You must come with me now."

"I'd rather take my chances in prison." Hands free, I tried one last cheap shot at the back of Andras's head, but the invisible binds immediately secured me. I yelped. Okay, I wouldn't mess with my demon friend again, but that didn't mean I'd cooperate.

29

A New Job

Malaikat

"Here we are," Andras File said with a friendly wave of his hand. "The customer service department. I think you'll fit in well, iKat."

"I think I will, too." I preferred the nickname iKat; it was less humiliating. Why my mother insisted on naming her demon son a translation of the word 'angel' always confused me, but since she died during my birth, I hadn't been able to ask. And that also explained why I knew nothing of the supernatural world I'd been born into. In fact, a lot of my past was hazy.

"Since you finished reading about recent events, what do you think of Nick Barnes?"

While pushing my custodian's cart through the halls of NBB Pharmaceuticals, Andras File had been the only demon—or human—who'd been friendly to me, and when he'd told me about this job opening, I jumped at the opportunity. Manipulating humans was a much more respectable job than cleaning their toilets.

I proudly gave my new friend a rundown on my studies. "Everyone remaining on the planet knows Nick Barnes is an eccentric megalomaniac. He was rich, and he loved attention, but he suffered. His family treated him worse than mine, and he was broken after he lost everything. The bacterium devastating the human population was his creation, and he was responsible for releasing it. In my opinion, he's a worse demon than some demons I've met." I beamed pointedly at my friend. "I don't think there's any way to fix him, and I hope he never gets out of prison."

Andras gave me a serious, unreadable face. I backtracked, "Was that the wrong answer? I can read the materials again."

Andras chuckled. "I hope you're right. I hope he's never freed." A slight mistiness settled on Andras's lower eyelid, and I thought the air felt dusty, but I couldn't see any. And why would I care if it was dusty at all?

Andras gestured for me to enter the spacious, bright room full of Desk Agents. Their clean, orderly, and bright working conditions made me giddy. I asked, "As a demon, how could he have no clue what he was doing?"

"Nick wasn't given all the information on our world beforehand. We all feared, and the king agreed, that Nick was more dangerous if he knew everything."

"Then why not imprison him sooner, or euthanize?" I understood euthanasia for demons to be a common solution to prisoner problems, a strange mix of a human's death row and an animal shelter.

"He had a very important job to do, but he couldn't get it done. Can I let you in on a little secret?"

I leaned in close, both curious and wanting to be in the trusted circle.

"All demons are immune to human disease." As that statement sunk in, Andras clarified, "Nick was immune."

Nick had taken the only prepared sample of Heromycin to save himself. "What a selfish bastard. Wait. Did he know, or was that something no one told him?"

Andras smiled, the tears glistening on his eyelids. I didn't have a handkerchief with me. I wore my very first suit to this new job, and it had a few wrinkles, since I didn't have an iron yet, but I was going to do my best. Like making toilets shine, I was going to improve processes, increase performance indicators, and impress the boss. I scratched my head. How was I aware of performance indicators?

"He didn't know," Andras said softly.

As a demon, it didn't affect me, but still I was angry with him. "Someone should've told him. Could've stopped this whole apocalypse in its tracks."

Andras gestured for me to move along, and he led me down a row of cubicles, where each demon stared at a computer screen, rapidly transcribing the standard reply for each situation. We stopped at an empty rolling chair. "This is where you'll work. The manual is there." Andras pointed to a binder leaning against the fabric false wall dividing the desks. "And your login name is Malaikat, password 666. Make sure you change it after your first login. The screen will walk you through all the prompts. Welcome to Hell."

I flinched. Andras's greeting sounded so familiar.

Andras rolled my chair out, inviting me to sit, and when I did, the muscled demon patted me on the shoulder. A small flash of something indecipherable told me that was a familiar gesture, too, but I couldn't pinpoint from where or why. Shaking off déjà vu, I grinned, giddy to have an amazing friend and new teammates. Now I'd be part of the coffee pot chat or the water cooler gossip. Oh, and I'd order takeout with everyone. And when someone had a birthday, we'd all share cake. For some reason, I really wanted cake.

Andras walked away, waving to a few demons as he went. I flipped open the binder, ready to read and memorize the whole thing.

"What's your story?" a feminine voice purred in my ear.

I turned, and a striking woman with black hair pulled into a sleek bun and a ruffled blouse rolled over to me. Her smooth, toned legs poked out of a pencil skirt. I loosened my tie. "Excuse me?"

"How did you end up here?" She eyed me with a smirk, pulling her red lips.

"Andras File got me this job. It's great, right?"

"Have you seen the latest news from the surface?" The woman pulled up a web page on her computer and turned her screen. "Look familiar to you?"

The Channel 9 news broadcast showed images and videos of plague-stricken humans miraculously waking up in hospitals and feeling better and hugging their families. I listened to the news anchor. "A terrifying bacterial infection ravaged the city. Survivors, and those lucky to have avoided it so far, still don't believe wearing a mask will help. Reports of missing persons have skyrocketed, and in related news, murders in the city have increased tenfold, with most perpetrators claiming self-defense."

I squinted and tilted my head. "Well, that's dark." Something about the story sounded familiar, though. "I thought the demon history covered this exact story."

"Nick Barnes," the announcer continued in the background, "the charismatic leader of NBB Pharmaceuticals has been officially listed as one of those missing persons. All attempts to enter his building have resulted in the conclusion that our rescuer has abandoned his mission. Anycillin is now Nevercillin." The radiant blond carried a sadness that I thought was more than just her day's assignment.

"Clever," I said.

The attractive demon next to me turned off the broadcast from the surface. "Our time down here is much slower than up there—part of why we live so much longer. Reading the entire history of the world can take years, but up there, it was only a few hours."

"Neat, but since the history was written by many demons over the course of centuries, and I noticed inconsistencies, how can we know it's accurate? Which recounting is the best one?"

"In the course of history, the winners of the conflict often transcribed the course of events and buried the truth. I can assure you, unlike the popular Good Book, ours actually happened. Minor differences weren't worth changing our amazing writer's words."

That term sounded familiar, Good Book, but since I never interacted with many humans—the closest I got was cleaning their feces—I couldn't figure out where I'd heard it from.

"I'm Heather, by the way. What's your name?"

"I'm Malaikat. Call me iKat, please."

Heather laughed—a full, deep belly laugh. I was used to the reaction.

After it stretched on, I said dryly, "It's not that funny."

I turned away from her and paged through the binder. This new job wouldn't be as easy as it sounded, but I refused to waste the opportunity. I shook the computer mouse and woke the screen saver. A suffocating, debilitating pile of filthy nasty buggers with their whiskers raking the air, clawing at the screen, tried to reach me with their beady little eyes and long teeth.

I screamed.

WITH NERVES SWIRLING IN my stomach, Andras unlocked a door identical to all the other doors inside Hell City's biggest apartment complex. So far, the only differing feature was the number outside the door, which I promptly memorized.

"This is you." Andras opened the door, and I followed him inside. "Congratulations on the job. I hear the interview isn't so easy. Mine was so long ago, I don't remember it."

"I don't remember mine either. Is that weird?" I said, settling my bag on the couch.

"It can be rigorous and forgetting is probably for the best." Andras closed the door behind us.

A single bedroom apartment just for me, not far from work. How much luckier could I get? It was furnished. I had died and gone to Heaven. Ha ha. Not really. Humans had that all backward, anyway. Hell was the place to be.

A simple couch filled one wall, and next to it was a large window overlooking Hell City, where the sun ceased to exist. The city's lights blinked, with people switching them on and off as they moved from room to room. With easy teleporting, no one had vehicles down here. The ventilation wasn't good enough for the exhaust, anyway. I didn't mind. It was so eerily quiet down here—peaceful. Across from the couch was a television, but the rest of the living room was wide open—the perfect place for a home gym and a saltwater reef. Not sure why I'd want a reef tank. I didn't know anything about them.

"What's wrong?" Andras asked, watching my face.

"Oh, nothing. I just want a fish tank for some reason. I think it would look great right along this wall. Don't you think so? And over here, I'll have a treadmill and weight bench. I hope these floors can support the weight. Hmmm."

Andras forced a smile and patted me on the shoulder. "I bet they can't. Lots of neighbors below you. But hey, the kitchen looks great, but if you don't want to cook, I left a stack of menus on the island. I need to get going."

"You just got here," I said. "I thought we were going to play cribbage."

"How about tomorrow night? I'll let you get settled in first." Andras's warm smile lit up his face.

I nodded. "Tomorrow sounds perfect."

Andras let himself out, and when the door clicked shut, I walked up to the wall and stretched out my arms. I bet a thousand-gallon tank could fit here, but how would I get it inside the elevator? Until I heard back about the floor's support capability, I'd start with a treadmill.

I shifted through the stack of menus. Tomorrow was going to be a big day. During the first day at a new job, everyone wanted to meet the new guy and see if they liked him. But on day two, the new guy was expected to perform.

I slipped the employee binder free from my backpack. I'd smuggled it out of the office, so I had more time with it. I sprawled it out on the kitchen island and sat down on a stool. I planned to be the best Desk Agent in the whole customer service department, and I wasn't against bending the rules to do it. When the king recognized my potential, I wanted a promotion. I was going to work at the surface as an independent demon without a boss over my shoulder, influencing humans directly as a Field Agent. After scrubbing their toilets for years, I was ready to show the humans what demons could really do.

I needed toilet vengeance.

Epilogue

Two weeks later...

Andras

I EXHALED A BREATH and braced myself. Angering The King of Hell was always a terrible idea, even by accident. And every piece of news I brought was always worse than the one before. I'd been tasked with giving Nick new memories, even though I wasn't a Memory Demon. I'd done my best, but after Nick told me what he planned to do in his new apartment, it was clear my attempt wasn't good enough. Hopefully, the king understood. I knocked and shifted my weight.

"Come in," the king called. The demon sounded in good spirits...for now.

I ducked inside the comfortable, yet typical, office. The king displayed his natural, red-horned self, sitting behind his desk with reading glasses perched on his nose. The chain connecting the glasses was strung around his horns, making him look like a sad Christmas tree. I closed the door behind me and released my glamour, stretching to my full iridescent dragon size. The news I brought was going to give the king a bad day.

"What's this meeting about, Andras?"

"I have discovered an alarming situation in the customer service department." Hell labeled the acres of cubicles lightly. They didn't have customers, and they weren't servicing any products or honoring any warranties. Instead, lower-ranking demons performed their agent duties from behind a desk, rather than face-to-face at the surface. One of them in particular I had been watching closely.

"Do tell." The king lifted his head from the reports in his hands. His short tail swished in agitation.

I shifted my weight again. "The memory wipe wasn't enough to contain Nick Barnes's true self. He's been filling his apartment with gym equipment and doodling fish in his notebooks between customers. The most alarming signs are the flashes of memory. I'm concerned keeping him in Hell will cause his memory to recover soon. I also believe having Heather work alongside him is hindering the spell's effectiveness. If Nick remembers what he did..." I trailed off, not wanting to vocalize the fear shared by all of Hell.

The king sighed. "In that case, call Wildabeast back. We'll have her fix it."

I smiled at the witch's nickname. I didn't know what transpired between the king and Wilda Rivers, but when they shared breathing space, they never failed to entertain.

"I contacted her already. She refused quite passionately. Her reasons included how you treated her last time, the fact that you owe her a favor already, and she has more important things to do in Bali at the moment. She also stated failure of her spell is your fault for not maintaining it properly."

The king rolled his eyes and tossed the papers on his hefty desk. "That woman is going to give me gray hairs." The king ruffled through the black wisps on top of his head. "If it weren't for Nick's aura heritage, I would've dispatched him already. We need Ronove's son to step up. He's our only hope. If being down here is causing his memories to leak through, then the only option is to send Nick to the surface. What would the demon think of a promotion to Field Agent?"

"I am positive he would be thrilled, but sir, if he remembers his past while in human form on the surface, with his new demon knowledge, he'll be a bigger danger than ever before."

"I'm aware, and since you couldn't control him before, you wouldn't be able to then."

I didn't appreciate the insult, but it was true. I had a soft spot for Nick. A weakness.

The diminutive king crossed the room and looked out his window. A vast city of lights glowed within the cavernous underground world. As if finding the answer in the depths before him, the king turned. "Until we can somehow force his cooperation, I have a plan. Has Nick done anything wrong lately?"

"I don't see how that's relevant."

The king sighed and pressed two fingers against the bridge of his small nose. "Your job was to make sure he stayed out of trouble. Has that been the case?"

I shifted my weight and swallowed. "Well, Nick stole from the office fridge."

"Great!" The king clapped his hands excitedly. "Bring him in for punishment."

"You want to give Nick a promotion and a punishment at the same time?"

The king smiled. "Sounds like a lovely afternoon, does it not?"

I didn't follow the king's reasoning, but to question him further risked my own hide with a trip to the dungeon. After spending personal time with the torturemaster, I had no interest in anything but casual pleasantries with the rainbow-colored demon.

"I will retrieve him at once."

Dear Reader,

READY FOR MORE DEMON Cat Chronicles? Get your copy of **Twice Curse**d! Make sure you collect your free copy of **Demon Experiment**—

Think Hell is above filing incident reports? Think again!

The exclusive behind-the-scenes report from The King of Hell, detailing what happened during the spell that "successfully" turned Nick Barnes into a demon.

What happens in Hell City stays in Hell City.
Kind of...

As an indie author, I'm thrilled you shared your time with me, exploring the crazy worlds and voices living rent-free in my head and keeping me up at night. Your reviews are very important to me, so if you enjoyed this book, please consider leaving some stars at your favorite retailer first chapter of Nick Barnes's story, **Demon Curse**.

If you found any typos or errors, I blame my cat. Rat her out at: support@stephanieflynn.com.

Thank you for your support!

Also By Marie Flynn

Demon Cat Chronicles series
Demon Curse
Twice Cursed

If you like steamy romance mixed in with your paranormal tales, check out Marie Flynn's other name, Stephanie Flynn!

About Marie Flynn

Marie Flynn is a pen name for Stephanie Flynn, and she is the author of the Demon Cat Chronicles and a big fan of the gray area between good and evil. She loves stories with supernatural beings who go bump in the night and some that slay during the day. She lives in Michigan, USA with her family and a small horde of Demonoid cats, from which she draws endless inspiration. **StephanieFlynn.com/marie-flynn-books**

www.ingramcontent.com/pod-product-compliance
Lightning Source LLC
Chambersburg PA
CBHW021127190726
48288CB00008B/2528